THE END OF EDDY

Édouard Louis

THE END OF EDDY

Translated from the French by Michael Lucey

Harvill *Secker*
LONDON

1 3 5 7 9 10 8 6 4 2

Harvill Secker, an imprint of Vintage,
20 Vauxhall Bridge Road,
London SW1V 2SA

Harvill Secker is part of the Penguin Random House group of companies
whose addresses can be found at global.penguinrandomhouse.com

Penguin
Random House
UK

First published by Harvill Secker in 2017

First published with the title *En finir avec Eddy Bellegueule* in France by
Éditions du Seuil in 2014

A CIP catalogue record for this book is available from the British Library

penguin.co.uk/vintage

ISBN 9781846559006

  Supported using public funding by **ARTS COUNCIL ENGLAND** ROYAUME-UNI

This book has been selected to receive financial assistance from English
PEN's 'PEN Translates!' programme, supported by Arts Council England.
English PEN exists to promote literature and our understanding of it,
to uphold writers' freedoms around the world, to campaign against the
persecution and imprisonment of writers for stating their views, and to
promote the friendly co-operation of writers and the free exchange of
ideas. www.englishpen.org

This book is supported by the Institut français (Royaume-Uni) as part of
the Burgess programme. www.frenchbooknews.com

Typeset in India by Thomson Digital Pvt Ltd, Noida, Delhi
Printed and bound in Great Britain by Clays Ltd, St Ives PLC

Penguin Random House is committed to a sustainable future for our
business, our readers and our planet. This book is made from Forest
Stewardship Council® certified paper.

MIX
Paper from
responsible sources
FSC® C018179

For Didier Eribon

For the first time my name said out loud names nothing.

Marguerite Duras,
The Ravishing of Lol V. Stein

One

Picardy

(late 1990s–early 2000s)

An encounter

From my childhood I have no happy memories. I don't mean to say that I never, in all of those years, felt any happiness or joy. But suffering is all-consuming: it somehow gets rid of anything that doesn't fit into its system.

Two boys appeared in the hallway, the first, tall with red hair, and the second, short with a hunchback. The tall redhead spat in my face *How do you like that, punk.*

The gob of spit dripped slowly down my cheek, thick and yellow, like the noisy mucus that obstructs the throats of old people or people who are ill, with a strong, sickening smell to it. Shrill, strident laughter from the two boys *Look, right in his face, the little pussy.* It is dripping from my eye towards my lips, ready to enter my mouth. I don't dare wipe it off. I could; I'd only have to lift my sleeve. It wouldn't even take a second, a tiny movement, to prevent the spit from coming into contact with my lips, but I do nothing for fear of offending them, for fear of making them more agitated than they already are.

*

I didn't really think they'd do it. Which is not to say that violence was something new to me, far from it. As far back as I can remember I can see my drunk father fighting with other drunk men leaving the café, breaking noses and teeth. Or, some man having looked too directly at my mother and my father, under the influence, erupting *Who the fuck do you think you are, arsehole, looking at my wife like that.* My mother trying to calm him down *Calm down, sweetheart, calm down* to no avail. My father's mates who would in the end intervene – that's the rule, what friends do, what it means to be a *real mate* – jumping in to separate my father and the other fellow, the victim of my father's inebriation, whose face was now all beaten up. I would see my father, after one of our cats had a litter, take the newborn kittens and slip them into a plastic supermarket bag and swing it against some cement edge until the bag was filled with blood and the meowing had ceased. I had seen him butcher pigs in the yard, and drink the still-warm blood that he was collecting in order to make blood sausage (blood on his lips, his chin, his T-shirt) *It's the best, the blood you get from an animal right when it dies.* The squeals of the dying pig as my father sliced its trachea could be heard throughout the village.

I was ten years old. I was new at the collège. When they appeared in the hallway I didn't know them. I didn't even know their first names, which was unusual in a small school like this one, barely two hundred students and where everyone got to know each other right away. They approached slowly, smiles on their faces, nothing aggressive about them, so that at first I thought they were just coming up to introduce themselves. But why would these older kids be coming to speak to a new boy like me? The playground obeyed the same rules as the rest of the world: the big guys kept away from the little ones. My mother would say much the same thing when speaking about workers *Us little folks are nobodies, especially to the fat cats.*

There in the hallway they asked me who I was, if I was *Bellegueule*, the one everyone was talking about. They asked me the question that I would repeat to myself endlessly for months, for years,

You're the faggot, right?

By saying it they inscribed it on me permanently like stigmata, those marks that the Greeks would carve with a red-hot iron or a knife into the bodies of deviant individuals, people who posed a threat to their community. Impossible to rid myself of this. I was shocked, even though it was hardly the first time someone had said something like this to me. You never get used to insults.

A feeling of powerlessness, a loss of balance. I smiled – and the word *faggot* that was echoing, exploding in my head went on pulsing within me, matching the frequency of my heartbeat.

I was skinny, so they must have figured that my self-defence capabilities were feeble or non-existent. At that age my parents frequently nicknamed me *Boney* and my father was constantly repeating the same witticisms *You're so skinny a breeze could blow you away.* In the village being overweight was viewed favourably. My father and two brothers were obese, as well as several women in the family, and people often commented *No point in dying of hunger, being fat's not the worst thing that can happen to you.*

(The following year, tired of all the ribbing from my family about my size, I decided to put on weight. I got money from my aunt and used it to buy bags of crisps after school – my parents wouldn't have given me the money – and stuffed myself with them. Me, the person who had refused to eat my mother's cooking when it was too greasy, precisely because I didn't want to become like my father and my brothers – which would leave her exasperated: *It's not like it'll clog up your bunghole* – suddenly I would gobble up anything around me, like those clouds of insects that can unexpectedly swoop down and consume whole fields. I put on nearly twenty kilos in a single year.)

At first they just pushed me with the tips of their fingers, not too roughly, still laughing, with the gob of spit still on my face, then harder and harder until my head was banging against the wall of the hallway. I didn't say a word. One of them grabbed my arm while the other started kicking me, his smile fading, taking his job more and more seriously, a more and more concentrated expression on his face, an expression of anger and hate. I remember: the kicks to my stomach, the pain of my head hitting the brick wall. That's one part of scenes like this that people don't think of: the physical pain, the body suffering all at once, bruised and wounded. What people think of – faced with a scene such as this one, I mean: looking at it from the outside – is the humiliation, the inability to understand, the fear, but they don't think of the physical pain.

The kicks to my stomach knocked the wind out of me and I couldn't catch my breath. I opened my mouth as wide as I could to let in some oxygen. I expanded my chest, but the air wouldn't go in, as if without warning my lungs had filled up with some dense kind of sap, with lead. They felt heavy all of a sudden. My body was shaking, as if it had a mind of its own, as if I had no control over it. The way an ageing body that is freeing itself from the mind, or is being abandoned by it, refuses to obey it. A body becoming a burden.

They laughed when my face began to turn purple from lack of oxygen (a natural response from working-class people, the simplicity of those who possess little and enjoy laughing, who *know how to have a good time*). My eyes filled with tears, reflexively, my vision became blurred as usually happens when you are choking on saliva or a piece of food. They didn't understand that it was because I was suffocating that I had tears in my eyes; they thought I was crying. It annoyed them.

I could smell their breath as they got closer, an odour of sour milk, dead animals. Like me, they probably never brushed their teeth. Mothers in the village weren't too concerned about their children's dental hygiene. Dentists were expensive and as usual a lack of money came to seem like a matter of choice. Mothers would say *There's way more important things in life.* That family negligence, class-based negligence, means that I still suffer from acute pain, sleepless nights, and years later, when I arrived in Paris and at the École normale, I would hear my classmates ask me *But why didn't your parents send you to an orthodontist.* I would lie. I'd say my parents, intellectuals, slightly too bohemian in their outlook, had spent so much time worrying about my literary education that they sometimes neglected my health.

In the hallway, the tall boy with red hair and the shorter one with the hunchback were shouting. Insults came one after the other with the blows, and unfailingly I kept silent. *Faggot, fag, fairy, cocksucker, punk, pansy, sissy, wimp, girly boy, pussy, bitch, homo, fruit, poof, queer,* or *homosexual, gayboy.* On some occasions we would pass each other on a staircase packed with students, or in some other place, in the playground. They couldn't hit me in front of everyone else, they weren't that stupid, they could have been expelled. An insult would do, just *faggot* (or something like it). No one looked over, but everyone heard. I'm sure everyone heard it, because I remember the satisfied smiles that would appear on other kids' faces in the playground or the hallway, from the pleasure of hearing the tall redhead or the short hunchback deliver a sentence, saying out loud what everyone else thought in secret, and would whisper as I walked by, and that I would hear *Look, it's Bellegueule, the homo.*

My father

My father. In 1967, the year he was born, women from the village didn't yet go to the hospital. They gave birth at home. When she had my father, his mother was lying on a dirty sofa covered in cat and dog hair along with the dirt from shoes constantly caked with mud and never taken off at the door. There are, of course, paved roads in the village, but also *trails* that are still heavily used, where children go to play, tracks made of dirt and unpaved stone that run alongside fields, paths of beaten-down earth that become like quicksand when it rains.

Before I started collège, I would go out several times a week to ride my bicycle on these *trails*. I'd attach a little piece of cardboard to the spokes of my bike so that it would make the sound of a motorcycle as I pedalled.

My father's father drank heavily, pastis and wine from five-litre boxes, as is usual for most men in the village. It's the alcohol found at the village shop, which also serves as a café and a place to buy cigarettes and bread. You can buy anything at any time of day, by just knocking on the owners' door. They'll always help you out.

His father drank heavily and, once drunk, would beat my grandmother: he would turn towards her all of a sudden and start insulting her, throwing anything he could reach at her, even his chair sometimes, and then he would beat her. My father, small as he was, trapped in the body of a scrawny child, watched them, helpless. He stored up his hate in silence.

He never told me any of this. My father never spoke, at least about those kinds of things. My mother took that on as part of what women were supposed to do.

One morning – my father was five years old – his father left for good, with no warning. My grandmother, another keeper of the family history (again the role of women), told me about this event. It would make her laugh years later, happy, finally, to have got free from her husband *Left for work at the factory one morning and never came home for supper, we waited*. He was a factory worker, he brought the money into the house and when he disappeared the family found itself broke, with barely enough to eat for six or seven children.

My father never forgot, saying in front of me *That fucking son of a bitch who abandoned us, left my mother with nothing, I'd piss all over him if I had the chance.*

When my father's father died thirty-five years later, on that day we were together as a family watching television in the main room.

My father got a call from his sister, or else from the hospice where the *old man* finished out his days. The voice on the telephone said to him, *Your dad just . . . – sorry, I mean – your father passed away this morning. Cancer. And also a hip that had been fractured in an accident, the wound got worse, we tried everything but it wasn't possible to save him.* He had climbed a tree to cut off some branches and he had cut off the one he was sitting on. My parents laughed so hard when the person on the telephone told them that detail that it took them a while to catch their breath *Cut off the branch he was sitting on, what a dickhead, how could anyone be that stupid.* The accident, the fractured hip. Once he had been informed, my father was filled with joy, he said to my mother *He finally kicked the bucket that piece of shit.* He added: *I'm buying a bottle of something to celebrate with.* He was going to celebrate his fortieth birthday a few days later and he was the happiest I had ever seen him, he said he'd have two events to celebrate one right after the other, two occasions to *get hammered.* I spent the evening with them, smiling like a child who imitates the state he finds his parents in without really knowing why (on the days my mother cried I also imitated her without under-standing; I cried). My father even remembered to buy me some soda and some of my favourite savoury biscuits. I never knew if he suffered, silently, if he smiled at the news of his father's death the way someone might smile after someone else spits in their face.

*

My father dropped out of school at an early age. He preferred evening dances in neighbouring villages and the fights that without fail broke out at them; rides on the motor scooter − *moped* it was called − out to the ponds where he would spend several days fishing; days in the garage working on modifications to the scooter, *tricking out his bike*, to make it more powerful, faster. Even when he was attending school he was in any case usually suspended because of inappropriate conduct towards the teachers, insults, absences.

He would often speak of the fights *I was one of the tough guys when I was fifteen or sixteen, always getting into fights at school or dances and my mates and I were always getting wasted. We didn't give a fuck, it was fun, and back then, it's true, if the factory fired me, I found another one, it wasn't like it is today.*

He had indeed given up on his vocational diploma at the lycée in order to start working in the factory in the village that made articles out of brass, as had his father, his grandfather, and his great-grandfather before him.

The village tough guys, who embodied all the much-touted masculine values, refused to conform to school discipline and it was important to him that he had been a tough guy. When my father would say of one of my brothers or my cousins that he was *tough*, I could hear the admiration in his voice.

One day my mother announced to him that she was pregnant. It was in the early 1990s. She was going to have a boy, me, their first child together. My mother already had two others from her first marriage, my older brother and my older sister – conceived with her first husband, an alcoholic, dead from cirrhosis of the liver and found only many days later, lying on the floor with his body half decomposed and crawling with worms, notably his decomposed cheek with larvae wriggling around and through which the bones of his jaw could be seen, a hole, there, the size of a hole on a golf course, in the middle of his waxy, yellow face. My father was happy to hear it. In the village it was important not only to have been one of the tough guys, but to know how to make your boys into toughs. A father reinforced his own masculine identity through his sons, to whom he was duty-bound to transmit his own virility, and my father was going to do it, make me into a tough guy, his pride as a man was at stake. He had decided to call me Eddy because of the American shows he watched on television (the omnipresent television). Combined with the family name he passed on to me, Bellegueule, and all of the past that went along with this name, I would thus be called Eddy Bellegueule. A tough guy's name.

Mannerisms

All too soon I shattered the hopes and dreams of my father. The problem was diagnosed early, in the very first months of my life. It would seem I was born this way; no one has ever understood the origin, the genesis, the source of the unknown force that got hold of me at birth and that imprisoned me in my own body. When I began to express myself, when I learned to speak, spontaneously my voice took on feminine inflections. It was higher pitched than that of other boys. Every time I spoke my hands waved frenetically every which way, twisting about, stirring up the air.

My parents referred to my *fancy ways*; *Stop putting on those fancy ways* they'd say to me. They would ask themselves *Why does Eddy always act like such a girl?* They'd tell me insistently: *Calm down, can't you lose the queeny gestures?* They thought I'd chosen to be effeminate, as if it were some personal aesthetic project that I was pursuing to annoy them.

And yet I too had no idea why I was the way I was. I was dominated, subjugated by these mannerisms and I had not chosen that high-pitched voice. I had not chosen my way of walking, the pronounced, much too pronounced, way my hips swayed from side to side, or the shrill cries that escaped my body – not cries that I uttered but ones that literally escaped through my throat whenever I was surprised, delighted, or frightened.

Every so often I would sneak off to the kids' bedroom, which was dark because we hadn't installed lighting in it (not enough money to install a real fixture, or some kind of ceiling light or even simply a bulb: a desk lamp was all the room had in the way of lighting).

I'd pilfer some of my sister's clothes and put them on and parade around, trying on anything that I could: short skirts or long skirts, ones with spots or stripes, clingy T-shirts or low-cut ones, worn-out ones, ones that were full of holes, lace bras or padded ones.

These performances, for which I was the only spectator, seemed to me the most beautiful I had ever seen. I found myself so beautiful that I could have cried tears of joy. My heart could have exploded it beat so fast.

Breathless after the euphoria of the runway show had passed, I would suddenly feel idiotic, sullied by the girls' clothes I had been wearing, or not just idiotic but disgusted with myself, stunned by the momentary fit of madness that had made me cross-dress; it was like one of those days when inebriation and disinhibition lead to foolish behaviours, regretted the next day, once the alcohol wears off and nothing is left of our deeds but a painful and shameful memory. I would imagine cutting the clothes to bits, burning them, and burying them some place where no one would ever dig them up.

Then there were my tastes, always automatically turned towards the feminine without my knowing or understanding why. I loved the theatre, female vocalists, and dolls, whereas my brothers (and even my sisters, in their own way) preferred video games, rap, and football.

As I grew up, I could feel my father's gaze grow heavier and heavier when it fell on me, I could feel the terror mounting in him, his powerlessness in the face of the monster he had created and whose oddity became clearer with each passing day. The whole situation seemed too much for my mother and quite early on she gave up trying to do anything about it. I would often imagine that one day she was going to disappear, leaving a note on the table to explain that she had had enough, that she hadn't asked for this, for a son like me, that she wasn't able to live this kind of a life, that she was invoking her right to abandon me. Other days I would imagine that my parents were going to drive me to the edge of a road somewhere, or to the middle of a forest and leave me there, alone, the way you did with animals (and I knew that they wouldn't, that it wasn't possible, that they would never go so far; but the thought did occur to me).

Confounded by a creature beyond their ken, my parents tried relentlessly to set me back on the right path. They would get annoyed, and say to me *That kid's got a screw loose, he's not right in the head*. Most of the time they would say *pussy* when speaking to me, and *pussy* was just about the worst insult they could imagine – that was obvious from the tone they used – the one best for conveying disgust, better than *dickhead* or *loser*. In a world where masculine values are held up as supreme, even my mother would say about herself *I've got balls, nobody messes with me*.

My father thought football might toughen me up so he suggested that I play, as he had in his youth, as had my cousins and my brothers. I resisted: even at that young age I wanted dancing lessons; my sister took those. I dreamed of being onstage, in tights, with sequins, and a huge crowd cheering for me as I bowed, gratified, dripping with sweat – and yet knowing the shame that such a dream represented, I never admitted to it. Another boy in the village, Maxime, who took dance lessons because his parents, for reasons no one could understand, insisted on it, was constantly being made fun of. *The Dancing Queen* is what he was called.

My father begged me *Come on, it doesn't cost anything and you'll be with your cousin, with your mates from the village. Give it a go. At least try, for me.*

On one occasion I agreed to go, more out of fear of the consequences I'd suffer if I didn't than as part of an effort to please him.

I went, and then I came home – earlier than the others, because after practice we were supposed to go into the locker room to change. I had learned, to my horror and terror (and yet it's something I should have thought of, something everyone knew) that the showers were public. I went home and announced to my father that I couldn't continue *I've had enough; I can't stand football, it's just not my thing.* He went on trying to convince me for a while, but finally gave up.

I was with him, we were on the way to the café, when he bumped into the president of the football league, whom we all called *Coach Cigar. Coach Cigar* asked, with the kind of surprised look people sometimes put on, one eyebrow cocked *How come your kid stopped coming to practice?* I watched my father lower his eyes and mumble a lie *Well he hasn't been feeling so great* with, at that moment, the inarticulable feeling that runs through a child who is confronted in public with his parents' shame, as if in a flash the world has lost all its foundations, all its meaning. He understood that *Coach Cigar* didn't believe him, so he tried to cover his tracks *And well, you know, Eddy's a little bit weird, I mean, not weird, but a little bit strange, he's happy just sitting around watching TV.* In the end he came out and admitted it, looking wretched and not wanting to meet the other man's gaze *I guess it turns out he's just not that into football.*

Outside my house, in the northern village of barely a thousand people where I grew up, I think it's fair to say that as a young boy I was reasonably well liked. Moreover, there were also many things that people associate with a country childhood that I enjoyed: the long walks in the woods, the shelters that we built there, the fires in the fireplace, the warm milk fresh from the farm, the games of hide-and-seek in the cornfields, the peaceful silence of the small streets, the old lady who gave us sweets, the apple trees, the plum trees, the pear trees in every garden, the explosion of autumnal colours, the leaves that blanketed the pavement, until our feet were lost, stuck in those mountains of leaves; the chestnuts that fell with them in the autumn, and the fights we'd organise. Chestnuts hurt a lot, and I would return home covered in bruises but I made no complaint – quite the contrary. My mother would say *I hope you gave as good as you got, or better, that's how you know who beat who.*

It wasn't unusual for me to hear someone say *That Bellegueule kid is a little weird* or to get smirked at when I talked to people. But finally, being the odd boy in the village, the effeminate one, I elicited a kind of amused fascination that set me apart, protected me somewhat, like Jordan, my Martinican neighbour, the only black person for miles around, to whom people would say *It's true I don't like blacks, there's so many around these days, always causing trouble wherever they go, wars in their own countries or coming here and burning cars, but not you Jordan, you're all right, you're different, you're all right with us.*

The women of the village would congratulate my mother, *Your son Eddy is so well brought up, not like all the others, you see it straight away.* And my mother would be proud and congratulate me in turn.

At school

The closest collège, one you got to by bus, nine miles away, was a large building made of steel and those red bricks that conjure up in the imagination the towns and working-class landscapes of the North with houses crowded up against each other, piled on top of each other (in the imagination of people who aren't there, that is. People who do not live there. For workers from the North, for my father, my uncle, my aunt, for those people, they conjure up nothing in the imagination. They provoke a disgust at daily life, or, at best, gloomy indifference). Those houses, those reddish buildings, those austere factories with their dizzying chimneys always spewing out a dense, heavy, bright white smoke, never letting up. If the school and the factory resembled each other so precisely, it's because they were barely a step apart. Most of the children, especially the tough set, left school and headed straight to the factory. The red bricks were the same, the sheet metal was the same, the same people they had grown up with were all still around.

One day when I was four or five my mother pointed out the obvious. I didn't understand, and so I asked, with that pure curiosity that children sometimes demonstrate, that abruptness that can force a grown-up to dredge up forgotten questions, ones that, being the most basic, can also seem the most pointless.

Mum, they stop at night don't they, they go to sleep, the
factories?
No, factories don't sleep. Ever. That's why your dad and
your big brother go to work at night sometimes, to keep
it from shutting down.
And what about me, I'll have to go to the factory at night too?
Yup.

Everything changed when I went off to collège. I found myself surrounded by people I didn't know. The things that set me apart, the way I talked like a girl, the way I walked, the way I held myself, called into question all the values that had shaped the kids around me, the ones who were tough. One day in the playground, Maxime, a different Maxime, asked me to run, there, in front of him and the boys he was with. He said to them *Just watch how he runs like a fairy* assuring them, swearing, that they were going to have a good laugh. After I refused he made it clear that I didn't have any choice. If I didn't do as I was told, I would pay for it *I'll punch your face in if you don't.* So I ran for them, humiliated, fighting back tears, feeling as if each leg weighed hundreds of kilos, as if each step would be my last, they were so heavy, like the legs of someone running against the current in a rough sea. They laughed.

From the moment I started at collège I would hang out in the playground every day trying to make friends with the other students. None of them would speak to me: a stigma is contagious; being friends with the *fag* would have been a bad idea.

I wandered without seeming to wander, walking with a sure step, always pretending I had something specific to do, some place to go, and I did such a good job of this that it would have been impossible for anyone to know I was being shunned.

This wandering couldn't last, as I well knew. I had found a refuge in the hallway that led to the library. It was always deserted, and I hid there more and more frequently, until soon I was there every day, without exception. Since I was afraid of being found there alone, waiting for the break to end, I was careful always to be digging around in my satchel whenever anyone passed by, as if I were look-ing for something, so they'd think I was busy and that I would soon be on my way.

The two boys appeared in the hallway, the first, tall with red hair, and the second, short with a hunchback. The tall redhead spat in my face *How do you like that, punk.*

Pain

They came back. They liked how out-of-the-way the place was where they knew they could find me without being caught by the monitor. They waited for me there every day. Every day I came back, as if we had an appointment, an unspoken contract. I didn't return in order to face up to them. It wasn't courage, or any kind of defiance that brought me back to that hallway – a short one with peeling white paint and the smell of industrial cleaners, like those used in hospitals or town halls.

There was just one idea I held to: here, no one would see us, no one would know. I had to avoid being hit elsewhere, in the playground, in front of the others, I had to keep other kids from thinking of me as someone who gets beaten up. That would just have proved their suspicions: *Bellegueule is a fag cause he gets beaten up* (or the other way round, it didn't matter). I thought it would be better if I seemed like a happy kid. So I became the staunchest ally of this silence, and, in a certain way, complicit in this violence (and I can't stop asking myself, years later, what the real meaning of *complicity* is, what the boundaries are that separate complicity from active participation, from innocence, from carelessness, from fear).

In the hallway I would hear them getting closer, the way – according to my mother, I don't know if it's true – dogs recognise the footsteps of their owners among a thousand others, and from distances that seem scarcely imaginable to a human being.

A whistling perforates my eardrums as my head hits the brick wall, and I can barely keep my balance. This is the period during which endless headaches would paralyse me for days at a time. Already, at this young age, thinking that my life was going to be short, I imagined that I might have a brain tumour (a young woman in the village I'd seen wither away. One moment thin and tall, then, suddenly, a few weeks later, losing her hair and putting on weight. More and more hunched over, soon being pushed about in a wheelchair by her husband. Misshapen and no longer able to speak, she would die during my first year at this school, the winter I was ten).

They grabbed me by the hair, always with the same relentless sing-song of abuse *faggot, cocksucker*. Dizziness, clumps of blond hair in their hands. The fear, therefore, of crying and making them even angrier.

*

I thought that in the end I would get used to the pain. There is a way in which people do grow accustomed to pain, the way workers get used to back pain. Sometimes, yes, the pain regains the upper hand. They don't get all that used to it, really, they work around it, they learn to hide it. My memories of my father who, caught up by his pain, would spend all night screaming in their bedroom next to ours because of his back problems, or would even end up crying, and the doctor who would come to give him cortisone injections while my mother worried *Where do we find the money to pay the damn doctor*. My mother was the one who would (also) say *It's in the genes, back problems run in the family, so then working at the factory just makes matters worse* without realising that these problems were not the cause, but rather the result of my father's punishing workday.

The women who work the checkout tills in the shops – because that was seen as women's work, men found that kind of thing degrading – who got used to stiffening hands and wrists, to joints worn out by the time when others their age are just beginning their studies, starting to go out at the weekends, as if youthfulness were in no way a biological fact, a simple question of age, of a moment in life, but rather a sort of privilege reserved for those who are able – thanks to their situation in life – to enjoy all those experiences, all those feelings that get grouped together under the word *adolescence*. One of my cousins was a checkout girl, in the same way that many other girls from our village and neighbouring villages became checkout girls, and would tell me, at the age of twenty-five, that she was already worn out *I can't take any more. I've had it* without complaining all that much, really, since she always added that she was lucky to have a job, that she wasn't lazy *Can't say I'm unhappy, there's others that don't have any work or whose jobs are worse, I'm no slacker, I show up every day and I always get there on time.* Every evening she had to soak her hands in hot water to soothe her painful joints, *checkout girls' hands.* Uneasy nights because of the way her body was sore and stiff *I'm sore from getting up and down and up and down.* You don't get all that used to pain really.

The tall redhead, and the other with the hunchback deliver their final blow. Then suddenly they would leave, already talking about something else. Banal, everyday talk – and noticing that detail hurt me even more: I mattered less to them than they mattered to me. I devoted all my thoughts to them, all my anguish, from the moment I woke up. Their ability to forget me so quickly hurt.

A man's role

I do not know if the boys from the hallway would have referred to their own behaviour as violent. The men in the village never used that word; it wasn't one that ever crossed their lips. For a man violence was something natural, self-evident.

Like all the men in the village, my father was violent. And my mother, like all the women in the village, complained about her husband's violence. She complained, in particular, about his behaviour when he was drunk *You never know what's going to happen with your father when he's plastered. Either he gets horny, and then he's a total pain in the arse, all over me, wearing me out with kisses and his I love you so much talk, or else he gets mean. That's what he is mostly and I've had it up to here, cause then it's like you fat bitch and you old bag. He won't leave me alone.* Sometimes, like that Christmas Eve when my little brother annoyed him by asking if he could change the channel on the television, his bad mood would turn into a kind of fury. On days like that he would stand up. Then he would just stand there, without moving. He would clench his fists tight and his face would suddenly turn purple. There's more: the tears that would fill his eyes (no tears for him unless he was drunk, on other days, he kept himself under control: be a man, don't cry) and the incomprehensible muttering. He'd begin by pacing, circling the table. Not the pacing of somebody killing time or thinking something over, but the pacing of a man who doesn't know what to do with his anger. Then he would head towards a wall, seemingly at random, and punch it hard with his fist. After twenty years of this, the walls were full of holes. My mother would cover them up with drawings that my little brother and sister would bring home from preschool. His fingers, brown from the clay walls, would start to bleed. He would apologise *Lot of good it does getting mad, no reason for you to get scared, don't be scared of me, I love you, you're my kids and my wife, don't you worry, I only ever punch the walls, I won't ever punch my wife or my kids, I might fuck up all the walls of the house, but I won't do what my dickhead of a father did, and mess with the faces in my family.*

His obsessive need to distance himself from the image of his father led him to have a lot of problems with my big brother, who was violent himself, even with people close to him. My father judged him harshly for this, with hatred even. Once my big brother got his mechanics BEP, a certificate for training factory workers, he dropped out of school and rapidly took to drink. He was a seriously *mean drunk*.

We learned this from one of the girls he had been hanging out with for a few months. She called my parents in the middle of the night and let the phone ring until they woke up. My mother answered. I heard her – there weren't any doors – talking in the kitchen (family room, dining room . . .). She kept asking for things to be repeated, and was getting angry. *What did you say, what, say it again, I can't believe it, what an idiot*. Followed by various shouts and interjections.

She called my father, stunned, shocked. This was the first time it happened, the first in an endless series, each time the same – down to the tiniest details.

She would shout *Get out of bed, he's made another fucking mess, but this time it's serious, really serious. He got drunk and hit his girlfriend and she was just on the phone telling me I'm bleeding, I'm all black and blue, my face is all messed up she said, Really I like your son, I respect you and don't want to cause trouble but this time I'll have to report him, I have to because I have kids too to think about and maybe him hitting me is one thing, but hitting the kids is another, I'm scared for them. You know your son gets violent when he drinks, he beats me, it's not the first time, but this time he went too far. I didn't tell you about it the other times cause I didn't want to bother you.* My brother's girlfriend went to see a doctor so he could officially report that she'd been beaten, that her body was covered with bruises. She filed a complaint and yet again my brother had to do some hours of community service.

My older sister had lived through the experience the other way round. It was like a mirror, there was a perfect symmetry reflected between her and my older brother, between the masculine and the feminine. She had started seeing a guy who lived a few streets over – girls in the village often end up with boys from the village or the surrounding area. He would come visit on a moped in the days before he got a car. Tough guys used mopeds to pick up girls, impressing them by doing a wheelie or a fancy skid in front of them, and then inviting them to hop on behind *Pretty hot bike I've got, right.*

Soon they moved in together, in a small apartment – still in the village, only a few streets away. He wasn't working. My mother couldn't stand the relationship, considering it indecent for a woman to support a man *She can't just live with some lazy jerk sponging off her, taking her money. He's supposed to be the man of the house.*

It was my mother who noticed that he was beating my sister. She was on her way home from the bakery where my sister worked the till. My mother thought she had looked strange, out of sorts, pale *She was as white as a baby's backside,* and she added *I think, I'm not totally sure but I'm not crazy, she's my daughter so I'm almost sure, I changed her damn nappies, I can tell when something's not right. I'm not an*

*idiot. I saw that mark beneath her eye, it looked like that jerk
had beat her up.*

The next day my sister dropped by to visit my parents.
She came over to watch a film and talk with my mother a
bit *You know you can't talk to men about clothes.* And indeed
there was a mark all violet and yellow under her right
eye. For a few minutes, when she first arrived, my parents
didn't say anything, but then my father said – or more
accurately, he *exploded* – but in a deceptively calm way,
without raising his voice, with a kind of restrained feroc-
ity, or controlled violence *What have you got under your
eye?* Then the panic in my sister's face, her stammering.
Even before she spoke a single word, we all knew she was
getting ready to lie. She said it was nothing *I tripped on
the stairs and ran into something,* before adding some kind
of a joke to hide her discomfort – since she could already
tell we knew she was lying, *I mean, you know me, I'm never
looking where I'm going, I can be a real moron sometimes.* My
father kept looking at her, more and more angry, less and
less able to conceal the state he was in. Fury contorted
his face, like when he punched the walls. He asked her
if she thought he was a fool. He said he didn't ever want
to see her again if she was going to stay with that guy,
and he didn't see her again for several months. We knew
he was overreacting: it wasn't my sister's fault. But once
again he hadn't been able to control his temper. In fact,
he hardly ever tried to do so, and moreover he bragged
about it *I've got a temper, you know, I don't take any shit, and*

when I go off, I go off. That was his way of being a man. He liked best of all the days when it was my mother who took the initiative, when she was the one to say *What can you do, that's the way he is, my Jacky, he's a man and that's how men are, doesn't take much to make him angry, and it's not easy to calm him down.* On days like that he would pretend not to hear, but a proud smile would play over his lips.

There was only one time when he found himself unable to live up to his role as a tough guy, during a fight that broke out between him and my brother, because, as I've said, it was a point of honour for him never to lift a finger against anyone in his family so as not to be like his own father.

We were on our way home from the fair that took place in the village every September (just one or two rides, not the big affair some people might imagine). Above all, the fair was the moment in the year when men could stay out drinking at the café until late at night without having to explain themselves to their wives, who, and this was a common occurrence when the fair wasn't around, would come and find their husbands at the café counter if they were staying too late *The kids are waiting for you to get home so we can eat and you sit here on your arse drinking away your paycheque.*

On this night of the fair my father had stayed late at the café with my older brother and also with my other brother, the younger one.

I wasn't with them because I hated it there, the men sitting around drunk and discussing the news and the village gossip. Their breath stank of wine when they spoke to me, spraying my face with drops of spittle, the way drunk men do, and every time, almost without exception, they ended up talking about their hatred of gay people.

My father and my older brother were drinking together when suddenly my younger brother disappeared. They started calling his name. At first they weren't worried, they told themselves he had probably just gone to set off some firecrackers near where the rides were, as they themselves had done years ago. All these experiences that the people living in the village reproduced exactly from generation to generation, and their resistance to any kind of change *That's the only way to really have any kind of fun.*

Slowly everyone went home from the fair and from the café as well. Only a handful of people were left. At that point my father and my big brother began looking around in the dark where the odours given off by the surrounding forest were starting to re-emerge: a scent of damp, fresh earth, mushrooms, pine trees. They yelled his name *Rudy, Rudy* without any answer. They began asking around *Have you seen him?* immediately setting off a huge search involving everyone who was still there. Off they went, spreading out through the streets of the village over which floated, like an echo, his name *Rudy, Rudy.* His name popped up, blossomed, from every corner. The entire village began singing the name and each call of *Rudy* gave rise to others, over and over.

My father was worried because of all the stories of kidnappings he had seen on television. Paedophilia was a myth that tormented the village. Once when a news programme on TV described a case of paedophilia in the North, not far from us, my parents refused to let me out of the house for several days. *They should cut the balls off fuckers like that and make them eat them, and then kill them, where's the death penalty when you need it, why did they do away with it, how fucked up was that, that's why there's so many more rapists around these days* and then my mother *No kidding, beats me why they don't kill people like that.* My mother had joined the search party, weeping and yelling *My boy, what's happened to him, don't let him be kidnapped, there's more and more men kidnapping boys now and then they rape them and kill them.*

Finally someone called out to us.

My little brother was sitting on the steps in front of our house. He explained that he was tired and had come here to rest and wait for the others to come home. My parents were crying. They took him in their arms and told him never to do that again. My brother, the older one, blew up. He had had far too much to drink. He started yelling questions at my little brother; why had he done that? My little brother didn't say anything, paralysed in front of this huge monster of flesh, my big brother, six foot three, a hundred and ten kilos, not just a double, but a triple chin that wobbled around when he spoke. He started yelling at my parents, accusing them of being too soft on him *Take a belt to him, give him a hiding he won't forget, that's how you have to do it, that's the only way you'll ever make someone a man.* He couldn't shut up, or get control of himself, he went on insisting that when he was a kid he got slapped whenever he was out of line, that he hadn't been raised like this. *What's worse, our whole fucking life was nothing like this. We had no fucking money, and all the time we had to humiliate ourselves asking for credit or going to the food bank for food.*

(We would go there once a month, it was true, to collect the boxes of food they gave out to the poorest families. The volunteers grew to recognise me and, when we arrived, they would slip me a few extra chocolate bars beyond our allotted share *There's our little Eddy, how's he doing?* and my parents would then tell me to keep my mouth shut *You don't tell anyone, no one, that we go to the food bank, that's a secret that stays in the family.* They didn't realise that I'd already understood, without being told, how shameful this was, and that nothing would have made me tell anyone about it.)

To the fucking food bank, or when day after day we ate the fish Dad caught because we couldn't afford meat, these brats never knew anything like that. That we even had to go out and beg on the street. He was lying, the alcohol was making him lie. He had never had to beg. *We got raised the hard way, not like these spoiled brats, and when we did something wrong no way we got away with it, we never got off so easy. And look at what happens.* He turned towards me, his eyes bloodshot, spit running down his cheeks, belching, about to vomit each time he opened his mouth. *Look at Eddy, how you've brought him up, what he's turned into. He acts like a fucking pussy.*

I pretended to be shocked, as I always did, so that others might think this was the first time I'd ever heard anything like this. A misdiagnosis. My brother must be out of his mind and if my mother or father had ever had the same thought, then his craziness must run in the family.

He wanted to make sure that my little brother didn't turn out like me, a pussy. And in fact I had worried about the same thing. My big brother couldn't have known, but I didn't want Rudy to get beaten up at school and I was obsessed by the need to make sure that he turned out straight. I had begun working on this when he was extremely young: I told him over and over again that boys liked girls, sometimes I even told him that homosexuality was disgusting, *totally sick*, and that it could lead to damnation, hell, and disease.

All at once he ran towards me, yelling *I'm taking you out, I'm gonna kill you.* My mother rushed in to protect me. Telling this story, she will say that she doesn't let people mess with her, just because she's a woman doesn't mean she gets scared. *Men don't scare me, still, he's a big guy, your brother, a big, strapping guy, but I'm not like some people who don't have any balls and just stand there doing nothing.*

She got between us and held him back before he had time to hit me. She tried to shut him up, shouting even louder than he was to cover up his hollering, so loud that it made her hoarse. *No way, you don't touch your younger brother, you don't hurt him, as if we don't have enough problems without you going after your younger brother. Calm down, calm down. And another thing, don't go telling me how to raise my kids, I raised five of them and I'm not having you come and tell me what I should or shouldn't do, go have some of your own and then we'll talk.* My brother was staring straight at me with his fists up, trying to push my mother aside, but she fought back. Because my mother was standing in his way, he started shoving her, calmly at first, then more violently, or, at least, with more and more force. *Leave your brother alone, leave your brother alone.* He raised his hand to hit her. Then it was my father who, in turn, stepped between them. I couldn't say what he had been doing during the time my mother was holding my brother back. I imagine he was yelling like her, trying to get him to stop. He must have been thinking my mother would be better at calming him down. He thought women were naturally better peacemakers than men, as shown by all the times that women separated their husbands who had got into fights outside the café (*That's enough now, enough of this foolishness, stop punching each other in the face,* and the husbands who went on yelling at each other as their wives held their arms back *I'm gonna beat him to a pulp, I'm gonna mess him up* until finally they came to their senses and said to their wives *Sorry babe, sorry, I got carried away, but that guy had it coming, he really had it coming, I couldn't just let him mess with me*).

My father pulled my brother aside just in time to stop him from hitting my mother. It wasn't so much anger as it was this unthinkable chain of events that made him ask my brother what was the matter with him, why he wanted to kill me and attack his own mother. Then he started begging him to back off; I was watching this transpire in a state of shock and incomprehension: I wasn't used to seeing my father begging anyone for anything, least of all his own children, whom he was always reminding of his authority *Under this roof I'm the boss.* He begged him to relax and tried to reassure him: he'd been brought up just like the younger kids, they'd all been raised the same way. He swore we had been given no special privileges *Never treated any of you any different* even if he wasn't the *biological father* of my older brother and my older sister. He told him he had loved them just as much as us *And when we had Eddy, other folks, people in my family would say to me you must be proud Jacky, your first kid and what's more it's a boy, but I said back, No, no. Eddy's not my first kid, cause I have two others that are older, and they aren't stepchildren. You either have kids all the way or you don't, there's no such thing as half a kid. It doesn't exist.*

My big brother Vincent wasn't listening. He wouldn't be diverted, he kept yelling, stammering, hurling all kinds of insults at me during my father's little speech. He had had enough. He wanted to have his way, he was out to get me. My mother sensed this change in him, this sudden desire to accelerate the action (telling this story: *Right then I saw things were taking a turn for the worse, who knows Vincent better than me, I brought him into the world*), she told me to go hide in the bathroom and lock the door *Eddy quick run hide in the bathroom and lock the door.* Vincent's impatience won out. He hit my father. My father didn't want to fight back, he refused, not wanting to hit his own son. He had slapped him now and then, the way he slapped me, as a punishment, when my brother had talked back, as a *rebellious teenager* . . . but wouldn't hit him in this context, he wouldn't get into an actual fight with his son. For a while he just took what was coming, only trying to hold him back a bit, to deflect the blows as best he could. I was hiding in the bathroom, so didn't see any of this. My mother told me about it the next day.

Then came the fight. My father was forced to defend himself. I heard voices all mixed together, my mother pleading with my brother not to hit his father, to cut it out, and then my father, at his wits' end, in tears, who could do no more than ask his opponent between two cries of pain (his back problems) *What do you think you're doing? What's going on?* Finally Vincent *You aren't my fucking parents, you can go to hell for all I care, just go to fucking hell.*

Then I didn't hear Vincent any more. He had run away once he understood the seriousness of the situation. When I came out of the bathroom my father was down on the ground sobbing. He couldn't stand up; he couldn't even move. I saw the tightness in his immobilised body, especially in his eyes, which is where the tightness appears in a body that has suddenly been paralysed, I saw him struggling to get up *Shit, I'm never gonna walk again in my life, I can tell, I'm screwed, I can tell.* My mother was panting, panicked, horrified, it was as if I could still see Vincent's shadow in her face as she asked me to help her pick up my father. I had plenty of experience carrying my paralysed uncle when he fell out of his hospital bed. Pick up his legs while someone else picks up his arms. We tried to pick him up but we couldn't. *He's heavy as an ox,* my mother was saying. He let out cries of pain whenever we moved his body even a little bit.

My mother told me that we needed to call the doctor, we had no choice, my father's back had gone out and she knew it, the only thing that could help were his shots.

It was barely an hour later that the doctor showed up. He gave him some injections just as my mother had predicted. My father stayed lying down in the same position for more than ten days, and the doctor would come back every day to give him an injection and reassure him, *It'll get better Mr Bellegueule.* His reply, *I doubt it, Doc, I pretty*

much doubt it, either I'll be here the rest of my life like a vegeta-
ble or else this is it.

One afternoon while my father was waiting for the doctor, my mother let me know he wanted to tell me something. I was taken aback, accustomed as I was to the silence that existed between us. She sounded surprised too, and looked up to the sky. I went into the bedroom.

I walked up to the bed. My father held out something to me, a ring, his wedding ring. He asked me to put it on, to take care of it *Because I can tell, I have to tell you, your dad is dying, I can tell I won't be able to hold on much longer. Something else I need to say, it's that I love you, that you're my son, no matter what, you're my first kid.* I did not find this, as one might have expected, beautiful and moving. His *I love you* had repulsed me, the words had an incestuous feel to them.

Portrait of my mother in the morning

Now my mother. She couldn't see what was happening to me at school. Sometimes in a detached and distant way she asked me how my day had gone. She didn't do that often, it wasn't her style. She was a mother almost in spite of herself, one of those mothers who had become a mother too soon. She was seventeen when she got pregnant. Her parents told her that her behaviour wasn't very grown up and that she'd been careless *Should've paid more attention*. She was obliged to break off the courses she was taking to get a diploma in cooking and leave the lycée without a qualification. *I had to drop out, but I wasn't useless, I was really smart, and I could've gone far, finished my certificate and done other stuff after that.*

In the village it's as if women have babies in order to become women, as if they can't be women otherwise. People take them for lesbians, or frigid.

The other women are always discussing this topic out-side the school *That one hasn't had any kids yet, it's not normal, there's something wrong with her, she must be a dyke. Or frigid, she's never had a good lay.*

Much later I would come to understand that in other places an accomplished woman is one who knows how to take care of herself, to look out for herself, for her career, who doesn't rush into having children when she's too young. It might even be all right for her to experiment with being a lesbian as a teenager, not for too long, but for a week or two, for a few days, just for fun.

My sister, who is direct and very tough (she needed a strong disposition, just as my mother did, to survive in a man's world), would complain that my mother had never been maternal, that they never spent time one on one, that my mother never took her shopping, or did any of the other things that mothers and daughters were supposed to do together. And my mother, because she was ashamed, would get angry, ending the conversation *Give me a fuck-ing break* or else she wouldn't say anything in front of my sister, but then later she'd tell me in private that she didn't understand why my sister was so *mean* to her, that she would have liked to take her shopping, but that – *and your sister knows all this, we live in the same damn house, and she's not stupid* – she was too exhausted with everything that had to be done around the house, with her little brother and sister to take care of, meals to fix, a house to clean, and in any case what would the point have been, spending their days in the shops when she couldn't have bought anything anyway.

My mother smoked a lot in the mornings. I suffered from asthma, and sometimes I would have terrible attacks that left me more dead than alive. Some days I couldn't go to sleep without thinking I would never wake up again; it took enormous and indescribable efforts for me to fill my lungs with a little oxygen. If I told my mother that cigarette smoke made it harder for me to breathe, she would blow up *They tell us we all have to stop smoking, but all that shit, all that smoke that spews out of the factory and that we all have to breathe, it's no better for you than this, these cigarettes aren't the real problem, they don't make any difference.* She was easily annoyed and always losing her temper.

She was often angry. She'd take any occasion to voice her indignation, railing, day in, day out, against the politicians, against the new regulations reducing benefits, against the powers that be, which she hated from the deepest fibres of her being. And yet she would not hesitate to invoke those same powers she otherwise so hated when she felt ruthlessness was called for: ruthlessness in dealing with Arabs, with alcohol, with drugs, with any kind of sexual behaviour she didn't approve of. She would often remark that *What we need is some law and order in this country.*

46

Years later, while reading the biography of Marie-Antoinette by Stefan Zweig, I will remember the people who lived in the village where I grew up, my mother in particular, when Zweig speaks of all the furious women, worn out by hunger and poverty, who, in 1789, descended upon Versailles to protest and who, at the sight of the monarch, spontaneously cried out *Long live the King!*: their bodies – which had spoken for them – torn between absolute submission to power and an enduring sense of revolt.

Although she is an angry woman, she is not one who knows what to do with the hatred that never leaves her. She rails when alone in front of the TV or with other mothers outside the school.

Imagine a scene taking place every day: a small square (recently paved) with a monument in honour of those who died in the First World War, similar to other monuments in other villages, covered in moss and ivy at its base. The church, the town hall, and the school form the borders of the square. For most of the day, the square itself lies empty. Around noon the women assemble there to pick up their children as they leave school. They don't have jobs. A few do, but most of their time is spent on childcare. *I take care of the kids*, and the men *they're at work* at the factory or elsewhere, but mostly at the factory that was the main employer for the village, the brass factory, my father's workplace, which regulated the entire life of the village.

*

Each morning she turned on the TV. Every morning was the same. When I woke up, the first image that came to mind was that of those two boys. Their faces engraved themselves in my thoughts, and, inexorably, the more I focused on their faces, the more the details – their noses, their mouths, their eyes – escaped me. All that remained was my fear.

It was impossible for me to concentrate and my mother could not – by which I mean, was really not in a position to – imagine that anyone could fail to be interested by the TV. TV had always been part of her world. We had four of them in a relatively small house, one in each bedroom and one in the only communal room, and whether or not you liked television was not a question that anyone ever asked. Television was something, like language or the ways we dressed, that was just taken for granted. We didn't buy the television sets; my father got them from the dump and then repaired them. When, later, during my time at the lycée, I end up living alone in town and my mother sees that I don't have a television, she will think that I've lost my mind – her voice betraying real anxiety, the palpable uneasiness of someone who finds herself face to face with someone who seems crazy *But what do you do with yourself all day without a TV?*

She tried to make sure I would watch TV just like my brothers and sisters did *Turn on the cartoons, they'll make you feel better, it's relaxing before school. I don't know why school gets you so worked up anyway, it's not worth it. Get ahold of yourself.*

In the end, these on-going morning panic attacks made my mother worried and she called the doctor.

It was decided that I would take a few drops of medicine a couple of times a day to calm me down (my father made fun of this *Just like in the loony bin*). My mother would say, when people asked her, that I had always been the nervous type. Maybe I was even hyperactive. It was just school, she couldn't see why I let it get to me so much. She would tell me that my being so nervous, my fidgeting in my seat, made her nervous, so she'd smoke even more in our little communal living area while I tried to focus on the cartoons. She'd cough, more and more violently, *I'll end up kicking the bucket if it goes on like this. I'm telling you, I can hear death knocking at the door.*

Sometimes I'd start trembling, shivers that went from the base of my spine up to my neck, movements that were imperceptible to my mother but during which it felt to me as if I were in the grip of irrepressible convulsions. I thought I could get time under my control. I would carefully programme each morning task (go to the bathroom, make some hot chocolate – with water if there was no milk – brush your teeth – not every day – wash yourself, but no shower, my mother had warned me. She told me over and over *We can't take a bath every day, can't take showers, there's not enough hot water. The water heater's tiny and there's seven of us, it's a lot, it's too much for a teensy little tank. And no fancy lip, don't you dare start talking back to me. You don't talk back to your mother, you do what she says. End of story. Don't go telling me you just go refill the tank after a bath and turn the heater on, I can already hear you thinking it, you think you're so clever. I know how you are. But just you think how much water costs, how much electricity costs, you know we can't afford it* – and then the joke that my mother couldn't help making: *There are bills to pay, and I don't have a boyfriend at the electric company.* On days when we did take baths, my mother insisted that we not empty the tub when we were done, so that all five kids could use the same water and not waste electricity. The last person – and I did everything I could not to be last – was stuck with water that was dirty brown).

Each of these daily tasks I would execute as slowly as possible. Anything that might put off my arrival in the playground and then in the hallway. Every day I hoped, but never really believed, that I might miss the school bus. It was a little lie I told myself.

A few times a month my mother let me skip school so I could help her with chores around the house *Tomorrow you're not going to school, you're staying home to help me clean the house because I am sick of doing all this housework on my own, I have to do everything. I'm tired of being everyone's slave around here.* She'd also let me stay home if I helped my father chop wood for the winter and stack the logs in a shed he and my uncle had built for exactly that purpose – northern winters, long and hard ones, required several weeks of preparations because houses were poorly insulated and were heated with firewood – or if I took care of my little brother and sister, Rudy and Vanessa, so she could spend the evening at our next-door neighbour's house. She'd come home with the woman from next door, both drunk and making lesbian jokes *I'm gonna eat you out real good you dirty girl*. Missing school was my reward.

Another of our neighbours, Anaïs, who always wanted to be nice to me, would come over so we could walk to the bus stop together. I couldn't find a way to make her understand that I hated her doing this. She forced me to hurry, when all I wanted was to walk as slowly as possible, making a few detours. Because she was a girl, it wasn't such a big deal for Anaïs to be friends with me. Girls can usually talk to fags and get away with it. The few friends I had back then were all girls. It was either Amélie or Anaïs that I'd meet at the bus stop or in the fields around the village where we'd play for a few hours. My mother found this disturbing (little boys should have mates to play football with instead of playing with girls), and would try to find ways to reassure herself and everyone around us. And yet I could still perceive something that wasn't really uncertainty, but more like a kind of uneasiness whenever she would talk about the subject. She would say to the other women, as if to banish her usual, private thoughts on the matter *Eddy's a real Romeo, he's always got girls around him, never boys. They are all after him. No chance of him turning out gay, you can be sure of that.* Anaïs, in any case, was a somewhat odd girl, who didn't care at all what anyone else said. She had learned not to care from hearing over and over again what all the women said about her mother when they gathered together in the town centre *Your mother will do it with anyone, she cheats on your dad, everyone's seen her sleeping with the workers from the town hall construction site. She's a whore.*

We'd be passing, Anaïs and I, in front of the factory, in front of the workers having a smoke before beginning their shift, or else on their break if they were part of the shift that started during the night.

They would be there smoking in all kinds of weather, in the thick northern fog or in the rain. Even if their workday hadn't really begun yet, their faces – their mugs, their sorry mugs – would already be haggard, drooping with fatigue even though they hadn't even started working. Still, they'd be laughing, telling their favourite jokes about women or Arabs. I would watch them, eagerly imagining myself in their place, desperate to be done with school as soon as possible, counting up – several times a week, several times a day – the number of years that separated me from my sixteenth birthday, when I could finally stop setting out for class each morning, imagining myself where they were, at the factory, earning money and not enrolled in collège any more. I'd no longer see the two boys. My mum couldn't hide her annoyance when I'd tell her I wanted to leave school as soon as I turned sixteen *Just so you know, there is no way you are dropping out, cause if you do they'll cut my benefits and that's just not going to happen.*

If, on those days, her most spontaneous reaction came from the daily desperation (money worries) she had to deal with, she would also, from time to time, let me know that she really wanted me to continue my schooling, to go further than she did, she'd practically beg *I don't want you to have to kill yourself with work the way I do, I just messed around back then and now I'm sorry, got knocked up at seventeen. Then the only thing for me was to work my arse off, that's all I've done and I've never amounted to anything. No travelling, nothing. I've spent my whole life doing housework, stuck at home, cleaning up my kids' shit or else the shit of the old people I take care of. I screwed up my life.* She thought that she had made mistakes, that without meaning to she had closed the door on a better future, on a life that was easier and more comfortable, one far from the factory and from the constant stress (no: the constant state of anxiety) of making sure she didn't mismanage the family budget – where a small misstep could mean no food on the table at the end of the month. She didn't understand that her trajectory, what she would call her *mistakes*, fitted in perfectly with a whole set of logical mechanisms that were practically laid down in advance and non-negotiable.

She didn't realise that her family, her parents, her brothers and sisters, even her children, pretty much everyone in the village, had had the same problems, and what she called *mistakes* were, in fact, no more and no less than the perfect realisation of the normal course of things.

Portrait of my mother from the stories she told

My mother would spend a lot of time telling me stories about various episodes from her life or my father's.

She found her own life boring and she spoke to me as a way of filling the void of her existence, which was no more than a series of boring moments and exhausting forms of work. For a long time she was a *stay-at-home mother*, as she would have me write for her on official forms. She felt insulted, sullied by the fact that my birth certificate said *none* on the line for mother's occupation. When my younger brother and sister were old enough to take care of themselves, she wanted to get a job. My father found the idea demeaning, as if it would call his masculinity into question; he was the one who should be bringing home the paycheque. It was something she had a fierce desire to do, no matter that the only lines of work open to her were hard: the factory, housework, or working on the till at a supermarket. She fought for what she wanted. In a way, she was also struggling against herself, against an elusive, unnameable force that encouraged her to think it was degrading for a woman to work when her husband had been forced into unemployment (my father had lost his job at the factory, I'll come back to this). After much discussion, my father finally agreed and she began working as a home aide helping elderly people bathe, getting around the village from house to house on her rusty bicycle, wearing a red parka of my father's from a few years back, now moth-eaten and, of course (given my father's size), too big for her. The other women of the village laughed at the sight *Look how stylish she is, that Mrs Bellegueule, in her great big parka.* When on one occasion it turned out that she had earned more than my father, a bit more than a thousand euros for her and a bit less than seven hundred for him, he couldn't take it any more. He told her there was no point and that she should quit, that we didn't need the extra money. Seven hundred euros for seven of us would be enough.

She spoke to me a lot, in long monologues; I could have left someone else in my place and she would have gone on with her story. All she wanted was a pair of ears to listen to her, and she ignored anything I said. I would turn on the television while she was talking to me. It didn't faze her; she just went on talking. I'd turn up the volume. It made no difference. My father couldn't stand it any more *Give it a rest, you silly cow, don't you ever shut up?* She'd drone on just like all the other women to be found in the village centre, to the point that a person might have thought that there was some kind of contagious disease they had all caught from each other. When they all gathered in front of the school, a string of endless tirades would arise, one on top of another, with no one actually listening.

Here is one story she often told to anyone who would listen: before she had me, she lost a child. It was unexpected, she lost the baby in the bathroom, just like that, with no warning, one afternoon when she was trying to clean the house, where it was impossible ever to get rid of all the dust because of the nearby fields and the tractors going back and forth all day, leaving mountains of dirt, the same dirt that sifted into the house, the crumbling walls of the house, and the despair in my mother's voice *No matter what I do, it never gets clean, why bother cleaning a place as run down as this dump anyway.*

He just fell into the toilet.

It was a story that, years later, she got a laugh out of telling. The laughter on her face accentuated her ageing, yellowed skin, her deep, rough, smoker's voice, a voice that was also too loud, so the others told her (and sometimes my father let me tell her too) *Stop shouting! Put a sock in it, woman! Zip it, zip it good.*

My mother likes a good laugh. This was a point of pride with her *I like to have a good time, I don't pretend to be a lady, I am what I am, ordinary.*

I don't know how she felt when she said things like this to me. I don't know if she was lying, if she was suffering. But why else repeat it so often, like some kind of justification? Maybe what she meant was that obviously she wasn't a *lady* because there was no way she could be. *To be ordinary,* as if pride were not the first manifestation of shame. She even said as much from time to time, *Look, when your job is wiping old people's arses,* that's the expression she'd use, *I make my living wiping old people's arses, old people with one foot in the grave* (then the inevitable joke, always the same one, at this moment of the story *All it would take is a heatwave or a flu epidemic and I'd be out of a job*), every evening *up to her elbows in crap* in order to earn enough to keep food in the refrigerator, the *fridge* (and all the regrets my mother couldn't stop herself from expressing *Five kids, I should've stopped earlier, seven mouths to feed, it's too much*). The difficulties she had speaking French correctly because of her disagreeable, humiliating experience at school *After your brother came along, I couldn't manage any more, and in any case it wasn't any fun for me.* She didn't always say *I could have gone further with my education, I could've got a qualification,* she would say, now and then, that in any case school had never really interested her. It took me a long time to understand that she wasn't being incoherent or contradictory, but rather that it was I myself, arrogant class renegade that I was, who tried to force her discourse into a foreign kind of coherence, one more compatible with my values – values I'd adopted precisely in order to construct a self in opposition to my parents, in opposition to my family – that incoherence only appears to exist when you fail to reconstruct the logic that lies behind any given discourse or practice. I came to understand that many different modes of discourse intersected in my mother and spoke through her, that she was constantly torn between her shame at not having finished school and her pride that even so, as she would say, she'd *made it through and had a bunch of beautiful kids*, and that these two modes of discourse existed only in relation to each other.

Then there was the shame of living in a house that seemed to crumble a little more each day *It's not a house it's a fucking dump.*

In the end maybe what she was trying to say was *I couldn't be a lady if I tried.*

She would tell me, with her voice getting louder and louder as she became more agitated (I'll have the same problem when I leave and move to the city – my friends from the lycée will always be asking me to lower my voice; I would find myself terribly envious of the calm, self-possessed voices of well-brought-up young men), she would tell me that all of a sudden she felt the need to go to the bathroom *It felt like I was constipated, my stomach hurt like when I'm constipated. I ran to the toilet, and then I heard the noise, plop. When I looked, I saw the little kid, and then I really had no idea what to do, I was scared, so like an idiot, I tried to flush, I had no fucking idea what to do. The damn kid didn't want to disappear so I took the toilet brush to try to get him to go down as I flushed again. Then I called the doctor, he told me to go straight to the hospital, that it might be serious, and he had a listen and it wasn't anything serious.*

She and my father kept trying to have another baby. It was a priority for my father *He really wanted a kid, he's a man, and you know, men and their pride, he wanted a family, he was always the favourite of his mum and his sibs, not his dad of course, because his dad was in jail, he wanted a kid, for sure, he wanted a little girl, but we had you, he wanted to name her Laurenne, it made me groan, no more girls, little miss whatever, and so we had you after we'd lost the other one. Your father took it hard losing the first kid, it took him a while to get over it. He couldn't stop crying. But it wasn't so bad, since I get pregnant pretty easily, I even got pregnant when I was using an IUD, and had twins* (my little brother and sister), *so there you go and, just between us, your dad is hung like a horse.*

That wasn't news to me.

I often saw my father naked given how small our house was and the lack of doors between the rooms. All we had were sheets of plasterboard and curtains to separate the bedrooms, we couldn't afford to install doors or real walls.

Then there was my father's lack of modesty. He would say that he liked being naked, and I held this against him. I found his body deeply repulsive *I enjoy walking around naked, it's my house and I do what I want. In this house I'm the dad, I'm the boss.*

My parents' bedroom

My parents' bedroom was lit by the streetlights outside. The shutters, which showed the wear and tear of many years and of the rain and the cold of the North, let in a dim light in which only moving shadows could be seen. The room smelled of damp, like mouldy bread. Thanks to the shafts of light one could see the dust drifting in the air, floating there, as if moving in a time of its own, a time that flowed more slowly. I could sit still for hours and watch it. My mother and I were close when I was very young: in the way they say little boys can be close to their mothers – that is, until shame came to drive a wedge between us. Before that happened she used to tell anyone who would listen that I was truly my mother's son, no doubt about it.

When night fell, an inexplicable fear would take hold of me. I didn't want to sleep alone. In fact, I wasn't alone in my room, I shared it with my brother or with my sister.

A room of about five square metres, with a cement floor and walls covered with big, black, circular stains from the damp that permeated the whole house, from the ponds that were near the village. The awkwardness felt by my mother (I say *awkwardness* so as not to say *shame* yet again, even if that's what it was) when I would ask her why she and my father didn't install carpeting *You know, carpeting is a good idea, we'd like that, maybe we'll do it.* Which wasn't true. My parents didn't have the money to buy it, or even the desire to do so. The impossibility of doing it forestalled the possibility of even wanting to do it, which in turn made sure it never entered into the realm of possibilities. My mother was trapped in this circle that rendered her incapable of acting, either on herself or on the world around her *We'd really like to install some carpeting in your room for you, but with your asthma attacks, it might not be a good idea, it's dangerous for asthmatics.*

I would hide the mouldy patches on the wall with posters of pop singers or of TV heroines whose pictures I cut out of magazines. My older brother, who preferred, as tough guys of course would, rappers and techno, made fun of me *Don't you ever get tired of listening to all that girly shit* (I remember one day, when I was going to the bakery with him, he spent the whole time teaching me how a real boy should walk. *Let me show you how you're supposed to walk, cause the way you do is just wrong, if my friends see us with you walking that way, they'll make such fun of my sorry arse*).

The bedroom was taken up with a bunk bed and a piece of wooden furniture with the TV on it. It was so crowded that you bumped right into the bed as you walked in, with only a few centimetres for your feet: all the space was taken up with just the bed and the television. As my brother watched TV all night long, I always had a hard time falling asleep.

So not just because the television bothered me, but especially because I was afraid of sleeping alone, a few times a week I would get up and go stand in front of my parents' room, one of the only rooms in the house to have a door. I wouldn't go straight in, I'd wait by the door until they were finished.

More generally, I had picked up the habit (at least until I was ten *It's not normal*, my mother would say, *there's something wrong with this kid*) of following my mother all around the house. Whenever she went into the bathroom I would wait outside the door. I'd try to force the door open, kick the walls, scream, cry. When she used the toilet, I'd insist that she leave the door open so I could keep an eye on her, as if I were afraid she might just evaporate. She got into the habit of always leaving the door to the toilet open while she did her business, a habit that later I would find repulsive.

She didn't give in immediately. My behaviour annoyed my older brother, who called me *Sprinkler* because of my crying. He couldn't stand the idea that a boy could cry so much.

If I insisted, my mother would always give way in the end. As for my father, he preferred yelling and being strict. It was as if they had divided up the roles that were both imposed by social forces larger than them and also consciously assumed. My mother: *If you don't stop your crying I'll tell your father*, and, when my father didn't respond appropriately: *Jacky, at least act like a father for fuck's sake.*

Standing outside my parents' room on those nights when, frozen with fear, I was unable to fall asleep, I would hear their breaths coming faster and faster through the door, their muffled cries, their gasps audible because the walls were so thin. (I would carve little phrases into the plasterboard with a Swiss Army knife, *Ed's Room*, and even, absurdly − given there was no door − *Knock on curtain before entering.*) My mother's moans, *Oh yeah, that's it, don't stop, don't stop.*

I always waited until they finished before I went in. I knew that sooner or later my father would give a loud, deep groan. I knew that groan was a kind of signal that I could enter the bedroom. The bedsprings were no longer squeaking. The silence that followed was a part of the groan, and so I would wait a few more minutes, a few more seconds; I would hold back from opening the door. The smell of my father's groan hung in the air of the bedroom. Still today when I notice that smell I can't help thinking of these repeated scenes from my childhood.

*

I would always start by making excuses, claiming I was having an asthma attack *You know that someone can die from an asthma attack, like what happened to Grandma, it's not at all impossible, not unimaginable* (I didn't say it exactly like that, but some days, as I write these lines, I'm too worn out to try to reconstruct the language that I spoke back then).

My father would explode with anger, and insult me. He didn't believe a word of these stories about asthma and my grandmother, they were just pretexts, *shit you made up*, I was simply scared of the dark, like a little girl. He would start asking himself questions out loud. He would ask my mother if I was really a boy, *Is he a fucking boy or what? He's always crying, he's scared of the dark, he can't really be a boy. Why? Why the fuck is he like that? Why? I didn't raise him like a girl, I raised him like the other boys. What the fuck?* You could hear the despair in his voice. The truth – not that he knew it – was that I asked myself the same questions. I was obsessed with them. Why was I always crying? Why was I afraid of the dark? Since I was a little boy, why couldn't I really act like one? And most of all: why did I behave the way I did, with my strange airs, the huge gestures I would make with my hands as I spoke (*big queeny gestures*), feminine intonations, my high-pitched voice. I didn't know where whatever it was that made me different had come from, and not knowing hurt.

*

(Throughout these years, when I was around ten, there was one idea I could never get out of my head: one night when I was watching TV – as I would often do all night long when my brothers and sisters were spending the night at friends' houses – I saw a news story on a weight-loss clinic for the obese. The young obese people had a support team that held them to a drastic programme: diet, exercise, and a regular sleep cycle. For a long time after having seen this, I would dream of a similar kind of place for someone like me. Haunted by the spectre of those two boys, I imagined teachers who would beat me each time I let my body do something feminine. I dreamed of getting coaching for my voice, for my way of walking, the way I would meet people's gazes. I searched and searched for such a programme on the school computers.)

Words like *affected* or *effeminate* could always be heard in the mouths of adults around me: not just at school, and not only by the two boys. They were like razor blades that would cut me for hours, for days, when I heard them, words I picked up and repeated to myself. I told myself over and over that they were right. I wished I could change. But my body would never obey me and so the insults would start up again. The adults around the village who called me *affected* or *effeminate* didn't always mean it as an insult, didn't always say it in an insulting tone. Sometimes they would just say these things out of surprise *Why does he talk like a girl, why would he want to act like a girl when he's a boy? Your son is a strange one, Brigitte* (my mother) *the way he's behaving.* Their surprise made my throat tighten and tied my stomach in knots. People would ask me the same kind of question *Why do you talk that way?* I'd still pretend not to understand, I wouldn't speak — then came the desire to scream, but I couldn't, the cry stuck like a kind of foreign body, burning in my throat.

The lives of girls, mothers and grandmothers

Between the hallway at school, my parents, and the people in the village, I was trapped. My only reprieve was in the classroom. I liked school. Not the school itself, not school life: the two boys were there. But I liked the teachers. They never talked about *pussies* or *dirty faggots*. They explained that differences should be accepted, they voiced the discourse of the French educational system, that we were all equal. People were not to be judged by the colour of their skin, their religion, or their sexual orientation (that way of putting it, *sexual orientation*, would always make the group of boys at the back of the classroom snicker, we called them *the boys at the back*).

My marks weren't very good. The bedrooms at home had no lights and no desks so schoolwork had to be done in the main room, where my father would be watching television or where my mother would be cleaning a fish at the same table and mumbling *You shouldn't be doing your homework at this time of day*. In any case, I didn't like doing homework, I never mastered what they call *the basics* because of my frequent absences, because of the language my family spoke at home, which was therefore my language, marked by frequent errors and the use of the Picardy dialect that we sometimes spoke better than standard French.

Still I grew attached to my teachers, and I knew that to please them I had to get good marks, or at least show them I was trying despite my difficulties. There was something suspicious about the way I would obey them: being an obedient student at school was considered girlish.

But only in the early years, after which the girls began to hate school too and to make trouble for the teachers. It was just a matter of time. Their elimination from the system simply took a bit longer.

When my sister was in school at first she wanted to follow a training programme to become a midwife, but then she let us know that she was going to become a Spanish teacher *so I can make lots of money*. For us, teachers seemed solidly middle class and my father would get angry whenever the teachers' union went on strike *They make money hand over fist so what have they got to gripe about.*

She was sent to one of those regular meetings with a careers advisor and she explained that she wanted to become a Spanish teacher in a college *But these days, young lady, careers in education are hard to come by, everyone wants to be a teacher so there are fewer and fewer spots, and the government allocates less and less money to education. You should pursue something where you have a better chance, something less risky, like a career in retail, and in any case, when I look at your record your marks aren't stellar, I have to say, they are barely average, you'd be lucky to succeed at the baccalaureate exams.*

She came home one night annoyed after one of these sessions, put out by the careers advisor's attempts to modify her plans *I don't know why he has to be such a ballbuster that man, I just want to be a Spanish teacher.* My father *Don't let some black man tell you what to do* (the careers advisor was Martinican).

My sister resisted for a while. The advisor called her in several times to talk to her. When she was in her final year at the collège, she was supposed to do an internship somewhere and the advisor recommended the village bakery. A few weeks after the internship ended she explained to my mother (who was disappointed: *We would've liked to see her get a better job*) that she no longer wanted to be a teacher, but rather a sales assistant. She was sure of her choice, the careers advisor had been right. An apprenticeship would guarantee her a paycheque, which she wanted so she could afford all the things she'd been deprived of throughout childhood because our parents had no money.

*

As I watched the playground monitor at school, I would try to imagine what she might have wanted to become as a little girl, before she was a monitor.

I never spoke to her. I did everything I could to keep her from seeing the blows I took from the two boys. To keep her from knowing that some people might think, did think, that I was a girlish boy who deserved to be beaten up. I didn't want her to find me in that hallway, curled up into a ball, my face begging for mercy – though, as I've said, I usually tried, without always succeeding, to keep smiling when they hit me *Why the fuck are you smiling moron, you think this is funny?* For then she might worry and ask me *Why do they do this to you?* And then I'd have to reply.

I have no memory of her name. It might have been Armelle or Virginie. All I remember are the nicknames people tagged her with *Loonytunes, Batty.* She would talk to herself in the playground or in the hallways as she kept watch. Mainly she talked about her grandmother, she talked and talked about her grandmother, obstinately, even when kids would say to her *Stop talking, no one cares,* she wouldn't even think of punishing them.

Her grandmother's story was the same as my grandmother's, a common story for grandmothers in the village, where there wasn't much room to be different.

Her grandmother suffered from the cold as winter approached and the days got shorter. She told her this the same way my grandmother told it to me: without really complaining, just making the observation sadly when she mentioned the cold that crept into the house, and her painful toes frozen by the cold.

My grandmother, who told herself that owning a house, *being a property owner*, as the ad campaigns or the politicians would say, would give her a higher social status, a better life, slowly realised that nothing had changed since she bought the house, and that everything might even have become more complicated because of the mortgage she had taken out and now had to pay off.

She's cold, but now she can't afford the payments for deliveries of wood. The man whom my father called *Mate*, who delivers wood to everyone in the family – he would drive through the streets with a small tractor loaded up with a few cords of wood – had stopped delivering to her *Cause I have children, you understand ma'am, I can't keep delivering if you don't pay, I have mouths to feed, I have a family.* As for the monitor's grandmother, she said that she used lots and lots of blankets to stay warm but it did no good, the cold got under the blankets, they were like blankets of ice, colder than the cold wind itself.

(My older sister, at the moment I speak, has begun taking the necessary steps to buy back my grandmother's house for a ridiculously low price, and my grandmother has left to spend the rest of her life in social housing.

She called me to tell me about it and to talk about the serious renovations that are needed, given the hovel my grandmother lived in, where the ceiling had a hole in it nearly two metres wide *And then you know I really love Grandma so I don't want to say bad things about her, but boy it stank in there. There were turds from God knows what all over the place, and mould. It's gonna take a long time to fix it all up.* My sister, who will never have been able to see anything but the village for her whole life, at the age of twenty-five already owns property that will need endless renovation.)

My grandmother, just like the monitor's, took in lots of dogs. It made her feel less lonely, and she could curl up with them at night to share a little of their warmth. *At least my legs are warm when I sleep with them, and they keep me company, otherwise I'm all alone and I get bored.* She adopted five of them, or six, sometimes more, and it really annoyed my father. He found her behaviour irrational, adopting dogs when she could barely afford to feed herself *And you can't even go out for a walk any more cause the dogs trash the house while you're out. You think I didn't see they've torn down the curtains, torn up the sofa, pissed on the TV. And on top of all that, like I said, you don't have the money to feed them.* She made excuses *They'll eat leftovers,* but – and everyone saw this happen – she bought food for the dogs and even less for herself. She was the one eating their leftovers, so in the end, she wasn't just cold, she was also hungry.

When my grandmother ran out of wood, she would head for the forest that surrounded the village. She would take her big green and blue shopping bag with her, riddled with holes, as she finally had to admit: *it's cause the dogs chew up everything.* She would scavenge for small branches to take home with her. My mother would do the same thing herself to have a fire in the fireplace or to cook meat on the grill when there was no charcoal, part of her maternal pride *My kids will never go hungry, they'll never be too cold.* To keep us from seeing it as shameful, my mother would turn it into a game. We knew it was because we were poor and had no money; children understand that faster than people think. My mother would say *Let's go collect some firewood, we could use a walk and it'll be fun.*

We pretended to believe her and she pretended to believe that we believed her.

Sometimes my mother would get tired and stop pretending. She'd give up all her efforts to protect us from reality and she'd make me go to the shop in the village to *ask for credit, ask to buy on account* what we needed to eat. *You have to go because if it's you who asks for credit she'll say yes because you're a kid, but if I go it's a sure thing that the old bitch who runs the shop will say no.* I tried to get out of it until my father intervened, *Get your arse in gear and get down there before I give you what's coming to you.* He was so terrifying that I would do as I was told in silence. Children are better at inspiring pity and I had been designated as the one most likely to succeed at that game in order to get us some food; it wasn't only the shop I'd be sent to, some days it was also our neighbours, or others in the village, to ask for some bread, a box of noodles, or a little cheese. The humiliation of the moment when it was time to pay for the groceries, and I had to say, but in a low voice so that the other women from the village who were there wouldn't hear *My mum asked could you please put this on our account* and then the woman who owned the shop taking great satisfaction in raising her voice so that, on the contrary, everyone would be sure to hear her words. *It can't go on like this, your parents have to pay because I can't just go on running a tab for them. If they're short on money they should work a little harder. Now you be sure to tell them what I said, I'm here at work every day at dawn, from eight in the morning till eight at night, that's the only way to get ahead. Okay, okay, this is the last time you can use your account, I'm warning you, the very last time, and only because I can't bear to see you leave empty-handed.* There I was, lowering my gaze, hating the shop owner, wanting to cut her face open with some sharp, pointed object *Thank you ma'am, thank you.*

Other times when we had no money we would eat fish that my father caught. He had always been a fisherman, it was a hobby of his; boys went fishing or else hunting. He went fishing all the time in the ponds near the village, even more after the accident at the factory that lost him his job. He would bring the fish home to the house and my mother would clean them and then freeze them, wrapped in newspaper or in plastic bags from the super-market. A horrible sight for me: opening the freezer door and finding these cadavers wrapped in a layer of ice. The most troubling part was seeing their eyes, imprisoned in ice after having been frozen by death. Then there was the smell that hovered about the family room for days after my mother had been cleaning fish. At the end of the month, when my parents didn't have enough money to buy meat, we would eat fish several days running. My disgust began back then. Nowadays my stomach is still turned by fish, a dish so prized in the social circles into which I wanted to move.

Village stories

We weren't the poorest family around. Our closest neighbours, who had even less money and a house that was always
dirty and falling apart, were the object of my mother's scorn
and that of others as well. Being unemployed, they belonged
to that segment of local inhabitants who were called *slackers*,
people who *lived off benefits, sat on their arses all day.* There is
a will that exists, a desperate, continual, constantly renewed
effort to place some people on a level below you, not to
be on the lowest rung of the social ladder. Dirty laundry
was all over their house; dogs urinated in all the rooms,
soiled the beds; the furniture was covered in dust, and not
just dust really, more a kind of filth that no word quite
captures: a mixture of dirt, dust, food scraps, spilled drinks,
wine or Coke that had dried up, dead flies or mosquitoes.
They were dirty themselves; their clothes were smudged
with dirt or something similar; their hair was greasy, their
nails long and blackened. Something else my mother was
always repeating, with pride: *Being poor doesn't mean you can't*

be clean, we may not have much money but the house is clean and my kids' clothes smell fresh, they're not dressed in filthy rags. Our neighbours would go into the fields around the village to steal corn and peas, exercising the necessary caution not to be caught by the farm workers, *keep an eye out for the yokels.* I spent a lot of time at their house, in the kitchen that smelled of kerosene because of the storage tank in the next room. It had originally been the room with the sink and bathtub, but since the neighbours didn't think such a room was necessary, they used it to store kerosene. We'd make popcorn from the corn they'd stolen from the yokels. And the stories we made up, as only children can: stories sewn together from lies, elements that were added or invented, exaggerations. Episodes in the imaginary life of our neighbour *And right at that very moment that damn yokel appeared out of nowhere and started chasing me with his tractor but I ran faster and faster and he never did manage to catch me.*

We would tell each other the stories that were going round the village and making life less dull.

One of those stories really struck me. It had to do with the death of a man in the village. He had no money left and had run up debts in all the cafés. My father likes to say that back then there were twelve cafés for a village of barely five hundred people. I say *a man in the village,* but I knew him well.

Loneliness and hunger – the old man must have been sick of his life. He was tired of living but he didn't exactly kill himself, it was almost as if even making that effort would have required too much of him.

But then people in the streets began to notice the smell.

I smelled it myself one day when I was out walking with my cousin. He said *It smells like something died around here.* I spent lots of time with my cousin. He needed me to tie his shoes for him or scratch his back: his disability kept him from moving normally. When he was a child, as his growth spurt was coming to an end, his spinal column kept on growing, grew in an abnormal way, up into his brain, causing irreversible damage. It was a serious disability. He walked crooked and the hump in his back distorted the clothes he wore. *The hunchback of Notre Dame*, the villagers would chortle. He lost his teeth at a young age; they started falling out one after the other when he was about twenty, and some days, for reasons no one really understood, his skin would grow yellowish, or even completely yellow. On days like that he had such a high fever he couldn't get out of bed, and it would last for weeks. He was disabled but no one in the village would say this word in front of him or his mother. We couldn't tell if his mother – my aunt – was pretending not to know how bad his condition was or if she actually didn't understand the situation. 'Parents are always the last to admit that their son is crazy.' I remember our amazement when one day, and it was the only time, we heard her say, as if she were confessing something, as if she were teaching us, telling us something we didn't already know *You know, my son is disabled.* When his mother wasn't around, on the other hand, the locals talked freely about his disability *Your poor cousin, how terrible, you're a good kid to look after him.* When I would go to see the doctor, he'd warn me *Spend time with your cousin while you can, you know he won't be around for much longer.* Then there were the jokes: *Your cousin the hunchback, the village cripple. The Mongoloid.*

There were more people with disabilities in my family than in others. Or maybe we hid it less, or had less medical attention, or didn't know how to handle it. Or perhaps it was just the lack of money for appropriate medical care, that and a hostile attitude towards medicine. There is my cousin born with a cleft palate, another cousin who is always getting sick and is allergic to antibiotics, to detergent, to grass. There's the aunt who pulls out her own teeth with a pair of pliers when she is drunk, for no reason, just for the fun of it – a pair of pliers like a mechanic would have. She is drunk often enough that, inevitably, she runs out of teeth to pull.

So on that day my cousin said, *It smells like something died.* He was right: something was dead. I wouldn't have known that it was the smell of death. The old man had decided to stay home, never to go out again. No more glasses of pastis, *a drop of the yellow,* at the village café where the men congregate in the evenings after work – or after a day at home, watching television, when they are out of work. He stayed home waiting to die, fixed, motionless in his bed. Rumour had it, I don't know if it was true, but they said he died in his own excrement. *He died in his own piss and shit*, but he wouldn't even get out of bed, he didn't go to the bathroom any more, he just covered up the puddles of piss and piles of shit with sheets of newspaper, a last little gesture to hygiene before dying. *They said his socks were stuck to his flesh, he hadn't taken them off for months, and with all the piss and the pus the socks just little by little began to get absorbed into his skin, glued on until they became like part of his body.* And then, silence. The process of the body's decomposition. The women of the village: *The worms were eating him*, and the stench that spread through the streets. A crowd gathered (it was the same day that my cousin had identified, albeit unwittingly, the presence of death – because *it smells like something died* was an expression we were always using to describe foul smells) in front of the house emitting the smell of the rotting body. Even though it was nearly impossible to breathe, the women used Kleenex to cover their noses so they could keep watching, so they could stay, so they wouldn't miss their chance to witness such an event, so they could escape for a few minutes from a daily routine that held no surprises, or even the expectation or hope of a surprise. Given his fragile constitution, my cousin threw up a lot in the course of the afternoon.

We told that story often, we thought it was funny.

A good education

My parents were making sure I had a good education, *not like the troublemakers and the Arabs from the projects.* Here was a source of pride for my mother: *My children are brought up right, I teach them how to behave, not like the scum out there* or – and I have no idea where she got her information from, maybe from things her father, who had fought in the war in Algeria, had said to her – *My children are brought up right, not like the Algerians, the Algerians are the worst, you know, if you look close you can see they're more dangerous than the Moroccans or the other Arabs.*

Having been constantly told by my mother that I was better than Arabs or than our impoverished neighbours, it was only after I left collège that I realised I was less privileged than I had imagined. I knew, even before then, that there were other worlds where people had it much better than in mine. Like the bourgeoisie that my father railed against, or the village shopkeeper, or the parents of my friend Amélie. It was even something I thought about fairly often. But since I had never actually been faced with the existence of these other worlds, since I had never been plunged into them, my knowledge was of the order of intuition or fantasy.

This is something I will discover much later, particularly in my conversations with my former teachers – teachers at the collège who were powerless, beaten down by the ways that parents in the village raised their children, and who would talk about my situation in the staffroom *Really the Bellegueule kid has a lot of potential, but if he keeps on the way he's going, not doing his homework and missing class so often, there's no way he'll get ahead.*

I belonged to the world of children who turn on the television as soon as they wake up, play football all day long in the quieter streets, in the middle of the road, in the pastures that lie behind their houses or at the foot of their apartment blocks, who watch more TV in the afternoon and evening for hours on end, between six and eight hours a day. I belonged to the world of children who spend hours in the streets, evenings and nights, *just hanging out.* My father – always awkward when it came to questions of schoolwork – would warn me that I could do what I wanted but that I'd have to face the consequences *Go out when you want, come home when you want, but if you fall asleep in school the next day it's your own damn fault. If you play at being grown up you get what's coming to you,* whereas the children of the teachers, of the doctor, of the grocer were made to stay home and do their homework. He might ask me several times in the course of a single week if I'd finished my homework. He didn't care what I answered, just like my mother when she asked me how my day at school had gone. It wasn't really him asking the question; asking it was part of a role he was playing, and sometimes the role got the better of him, against his will, as if he were accepting, or rather interiorising, the fact that it was preferable, or that it was more legitimate, for a child to do his homework well.

Going out always involved the bus stop, the centre of a boy's life. We spent our evenings there, sheltered from the wind and the rain. I think that it has always been that way: teenage boys gathering there every night, to drink and to talk. My brother and my father both put in their time, and when I've returned to the village I've seen boys there who were only eight years old when I left. They had taken up the place that had been mine a few years earlier; nothing ever changes.

We would talk on endlessly through the night: about what was going on in the village, as if it were a world unto itself, isolated from all knowledge from outside, from elsewhere, about pranks, the mailboxes we would kick over just for the fun of it, Jeanine, the old lady who lived across from the bus stop, and who would call the police when we made too much noise and we'd hurl insults at her *you old whore, you crazy old bitch,* before we ran away. We would buy cases of beer and drink until we were sick, videoing ourselves on our mobile phones.

I remember from a very early age, thirteen or fourteen, having to deal with people passing out, falling into alcohol-induced comas. Calling the paramedics, propping up one of my *mates* on his side so he wouldn't drown in his own vomit. When it happened to me, the morning after the night of drinking (we would say *Let's get plastered this Saturday again*), I would wake up in a tent we had made a point of pitching in one of the pastures around the village, with my clothes stiff with dried puke, in a dirty sleeping bag that reeked, almost indescribably, of the food that my irritated stomach had thrown up, my belly aching and my skull pounding, as if my heart and lungs had switched places with my brain for a day. My *mates* would laugh and tell me that I'd nearly died, that I could have drowned in my vomit, could have swallowed my tongue.

I tried hard to hang out with boys as much as possible for my parents' sake. The truth was I found spending time with them boring. And often enough when I told my mother I was heading off to play with them, I was actually going to meet Amélie. One of my favourite games was to do her make-up, using lipstick and all sorts of different powders. I hardly dare imagine the terror that would have gripped my parents if they had known. I felt a need to reassure them, to act in such a way that they'd stop asking me questions I wished would simply go away.

Fights were a frequent feature of these evenings. At the bus stop, cheap whisky and pastis joined the litres of beer. The festivities lasted through the night right up until the break of day, hours of free time, of waiting for the time to pass or really for it to arrive. It was also built from red bricks, the bus stop, and tagged *Fuck the dam pigs, Kill the fuckin fagots.*

Fights were par for the course; girls fought as well as guys – but mainly the guys, and not just under the influence of alcohol (almost every day in the playground: children grouped around two adversaries – sometimes more than two – screaming the name of the one they wanted to win at the top of their lungs).

Such a fight broke out one day between me and Amélie. It was about something childish. Her parents were better off than mine, although not really *bourgeois*: her mother worked at the hospital and her father was a technician for the power company. That day, to hurt my feelings, Amélie – knowing this would work – had called my parents slackers. I remember this fight with the precision of events in our lives we create out of memories that might have been banal or insignificant. But then months, or even years later, depending on who one becomes, they take on meaning.

I punched her. I grabbed her by the hair and slammed her head against the parked school bus, violently, just like the big redhead and the little hunchback did to me in the library hallway. Lots of kids saw us. They laughed and egged me on, *Do it, punch her, punch her face in.* Amélie, who was crying, begged me to stop. She screamed, moaned, begged. She had made me understand that she belonged to a more reputable world than mine. While I was spending my time at the bus stop, other children like her, Amélie, were reading books their parents had given them, were going to the cinema, even to the theatre. In the evenings their parents spoke about literature, about history — a conversation between Amélie and her mother about Eleanor of Aquitaine had left me white with shame — while they ate their dinner.

At my parents' house we didn't have dinner; we ate. Most of the time, in fact, the verb we used was *bouffer, chow down.* My father's daily call was *Come and get it, let's chow down.* When, years later, I say *have dinner* in front of my parents, they will make fun of me *Listen to him talk, all full of himself. You can see what's happened, he's gone off to that fancy school and now he thinks he's a gentleman, he's going to philosophise for us.*

To philosophise meant talking like the class enemy, *the haves, the rich folk.* It meant talking like people who have the good fortune to go to good schools and universities, and therefore to study philosophy. It is true, the other children, those who *have dinner*, sometimes drink beer, watch TV, and play football. But people who play football, drink beer and watch TV don't go to the theatre.

It was to Amélie that I would formulate my complaints about how, compared to her own mother, my mother didn't pay enough attention to me. I wasn't able to see that Amélie's mother had a different kind of job, a different status, an easier life. I couldn't see that it was harder for my mother to find time to devote to me and thereby demonstrate her love.

There were other occasions, of course, when I was grateful for my mother's lack of attention. When I would arrive home from school, she could have seen how drawn my face was, as if I had wrinkles. If my face seemed wrinkled, it was because the beatings aged me. I was only eleven, but already I was older than my mother.

Deep down, I know she knew. It wasn't a clear picture, but rather something she had a hard time putting into words, something she felt but couldn't express. I was afraid that someday she would manage to formulate all the questions that had been building up – in silence – over the years. I was afraid that I'd have to answer, to talk to her about being beaten up, to tell her that other people thought the same things she did. I hoped she didn't think too much about these things, and that in the end she would just forget.

One morning before I left for school she said to me *You know Eddy, you should really just cut it out with all the fancy manners, people make fun of you behind your back, I hear them, you know, and you know what else, you should lighten up a bit, go out and meet some girls.* She said this, in the way my father would speak, with a mix of confusion, shame, and annoyance. She couldn't figure out why I didn't try to pick up girls, like my father had done years ago, in nightclubs or at the dances in the village hall.

Starting around the age of twelve I would go to night-clubs with a couple of *mates* on Saturday nights in order to meet girls – at least that's what I told my parents, repeatedly, so that they'd be sure to catch the fictive justifications for these outings. My father, not as easy to fool as I had hoped, saw perfectly clearly that I never introduced him to any of the girls that it would be reasonable to expect I would meet in these places. He would wonder out loud why I was so passive when my brother would bring home a new girl every month, making introductions, and talking about engagement, marriage, kids.

(This was a privilege reserved for young men. When my sister, coming home from a dance, introduced her second boyfriend to my parents – having broken up with the first one – they told her this wasn't acceptable. She couldn't be bringing home a different boy, given that the whole village had already seen her with another one *You know the problem's not with us, he seems fine and we don't have anything against him, but you can't just bring boys home like that whenever you want. It's for your own good we're telling you this, cause other folks, you better believe it, they're just going to call you a whore.)*

If my parents seemed backed into a corner of incomprehension when it came to my behaviour, my choices, my taste, shame would often be mixed with pride when I was the topic in question. My father would never say anything but my mother would tell me *Don't blame him, you know, he's a man, and men can't tell you what they're feeling.* He would tell his mates at the factory who would then report it to me that *My boy is good at school, he's smart and maybe he's even gifted. He's smart, he's going to go on with his studies, and what's really great* (this is what made him happiest), *what's really great, is that kid will get rich.* He may have hated, as he often said, *bourgeois, middle-class* people as much as he hated Arabs or Jews, but he really wanted to see me pass over to the other side.

Coming home from school I would find him in our communal room slumped in his chair and drinking his pastis while he watched TV. The TV would be turned up too loud, he'd snore when he fell asleep in front of it, and insult my mother when she walked by and blocked the screen. His body's position was always the same: legs stretched out and hands on his belly. My older sister: *With his hands holding his pot belly it's like he's pregnant.* The room smelled of grease because my mother was always making chips, my father's favourite dish *I like eating a man's food, food that sticks to your ribs, not like that fancy rich people crap where the more it costs the less they put on your plate.* It wasn't just my *father's favourite dish*, it was also one of the few dishes he ate, one of the few we all ate since he decided what we'd be eating. Even if my mother pretended that she decided, she'd give herself away when she'd say *I'd really like to cook some beans or make a salad from time to time but your dad would throw a fit.* Meals consisted solely of chips, pasta, every now and then rice, and meat, ground beef bought frozen or else ham from the discount supermarket. The ham wasn't pink, more like fuchsia and dripping with fat.

So the room smelled of grease, of wood fire, and of mildew. The television was on all day long, and during the night when he fell asleep in front of it, *it's good background noise, I can't get along without the TV*, or, more exactly, he didn't say *the TV*, but *I can't get along without my TV.*

We learned never, ever to bother him when he was watching his TV. This was the way things were done when it was time to sit down to eat: watch TV and keep your mouth shut, or else my father would become annoyed, and demand silence, *Shut your trap, you're using up all the oxygen. In my house, I expect my kids to be polite, and being polite means you don't talk while you eat, you keep quiet and watch TV with your family.*

While we were eating, he (my father) would say something from time to time, but he was the only person who was allowed to. He would make comments about the news *Damn towelheads, that's all you see on the news, dirty Arabs. It's like we're not even in France any more, we're in Africa*, as for the meal he was eating *There's one more the Germans won't get.*

He and I had never had a real conversation. Even the simplest things, *Good morning* or *happy birthday*, were things he had stopped saying to me. On my birthday he'd hand me a couple of presents, without a word. Not that I was complaining, I didn't want him to talk to me. He'd explain in a falsely casual voice, one that did a bad job of hiding his embarrassment *We'll get you some presents on the first of the month, when the benefit cheque comes. Bad luck being born on the thirtieth of October, end of the month.*

I didn't know anything about him, nothing at all about his past; anything I knew I had learned from my mother.

Every night his friends would show up around six o'clock with bottles of pastis. My father wasn't working any more. One morning – or one evening, I'm no longer sure – he had left for the factory as usual. He had taken his lunch tin with him, food that my mother had prepared the night before and put into a Tupperware for the next day. My father ate straight out of the tin, like an animal. On that day, the factory called my mother: *Your husband's back gave out all of a sudden, he had tears in his eyes, and we all know Jacky, he can put up with a lot, but he was actually crying from the pain.* Then the doctor came on the line (or else it was my father himself) *Your husband was carrying weights that were much too heavy for him at the factory, and for much too long a time. He should have realised it sooner and taken precautions. (But you know, Jacky doesn't like doctors, he doesn't trust them, he won't take his medicine, just like his brother-in-law who's half paralysed.) His back is in bad shape, it's a mess, the discs are ruptured. He's going to have to stop working for an indefinite period of time.* My mother: *But if he's on unemployment that'll mean less money, won't it?*

My father came home that same night and for several days he didn't get out of bed. Sometimes his cries would drown out the sound of the television and of the crying babies next door. My mother: *That woman has no idea how to raise kids.*

He thought he'd have to take a short break from work, a few weeks at the most. Weeks soon became months and months years, and my parents would speak of *long-term disability, expiration of benefits, unemployment limits, minimum wage.* My mother finally admitted to me *Yes he could go back to work, your dad, if he wanted to, but you can see what he likes, drinking bottles of pastis night after night in front of the TV with his pals. You might as well understand, Eddy, your father's an alcoholic, and he's never going back to work.*

After several years of not working, my father had to face up to what was being said about him in the village, by the women outside the school or in front of the shop *Jacky's a slacker, it's been four years since he had a job, he can't even feed his wife and kids. Look at what a dump his house is, the shutters are falling off, the paint's peeling, and then there's his grown-up son who's nothing but a drunk who he can't control.*

My parents stubbornly refused to pay any attention to the gossip. My mother told me she didn't give a damn about the rumours *Those two-faced bitches, who gives a shit, not me, they can mind their own fucking business.* My father had in fact tried to find work, but had got discouraged around the hundredth rejection. He kept on inviting his friends over every night and they'd bring two litres of pastis, or even more, just for the three of them, and the more the months went by, the harder it became to get drunk. My father and his mates were perfectly aware of it *These days there's more pastis in my veins than blood.*

I would get home from school at nightfall every Friday. I was in a theatre group that my French teacher had organised: my father, who had no idea what to make of my interest in theatre, found this extremely annoying and would often refuse to come pick me up in the car after the class, grumbling *No one told you to get involved in this theatre crap.* I would cover the fifteen kilometres between school and home on foot, walking through fields for hours, with the mud and dirt that collected on my shoes making them kilos heavier. The fields seemed endless; they went on, as one says, as far as the eye could see, with animals crossing them to get from one grove of trees to another.

These evenings when I got home later than usual, my father's mates would already be there. They'd be drinking glass after glass of pastis, each time saying *Come on, just one more for the road* and my mother would retort *A couple more one mores and we'll be lucky to get you out the door on all fours*. The room was inevitably clouded with smoke from the cigarettes and the wood-burning stove, thick enough to dim the light. My mother: *Now that's a good smoke*. The television. My father and his pals, Titi and Dédé, watched the same show every night. Always the same running commentary about the women on the show in order to mutually reaffirm their virility *Damn she's hot, that babe, I'd like to have a go at her, I'd jump her bones*, and my annoyed mother *That's all these jerks can think about*. One time, when I got home from school, they had a different channel on. It was a rare occurrence given their loyalty to their favourite programme, *Wheel of Fortune*. They'd say, when it was time for the programme to start *Our show, quick it's time for 'Wheel', don't wanna miss the beginning*, interrupting whatever they'd been doing, or talking about, and rushing to their seats, breathless. They'd been waiting for this moment all day; in a way, the whole day only made sense as a prelude to this moment of watching *Wheel* in the evening, glass in hand.

There was a gay man on the other channel who was part of a reality TV show. He was quite extroverted, wore bright colours, had effeminate manners, and a crazy hairdo as far as anyone like my parents was concerned. The very idea that a man would get a professional hair cut was frowned upon. Men got their hair cut by their wives with an electric razor; they didn't go to a salon. This fellow really made them laugh – that laughter again – each time he'd speak *Man, I bet that guy visits the fudge-packing factory. Watch out, don't drop the soap! What, no way, he'd be the one bending over more likely.* This was the kind of humour that easily veered towards disgust *Those fucking faggots should all be shot, or someone should stick a hot poker up their arse.*

It was at that moment, while they were talking about the gay man on the television, that I got home from school. His name was Steevy. My father turned around and called out to me *Hey Steevy, how's it goin'? How was school?* Titi and Dédé guffawed, they were laughing hysterically: it brought tears to their eyes, they were doubled over, as if possessed, gasping for breath *Steevy, oh my God it's true, now that you say it, your kid acts kinda the same way when he talks.* Once again, crying was not an option. I smiled and hurried to my room.

My other father

Here is an anecdote my mother told me. It was during one of the village dances – outlandishly named dances that would take place in the village hall a couple of times a year, like 'Tartiflette and Eighties Night', or 'Cassoulet and Johnny Lookalikes Night'. There was a gay man, a brave guy, who had made the choice to live his life openly. He would go to these dances with other men he had met, probably at some of the cruising spots found in the area, deserted car parks or seedy petrol stations. All the boys from the village would also turn up, gangs of mates who came to drink, have fun, sing, and try to pick up the very small number of girls who weren't already taken, who didn't already have children. What with the alcohol and group dynamics, the boys started bothering the gay man, bumping into him with their shoulders, giving him hostile looks, *So what's your story, you're a fag, right, you like sucking dick, stop looking at me like that or I'll punch your face in.* My father came over, having heard everything. He was really angry, his jaw clenched, and he said, *Leave him the fuck alone, you shitheads, you think you're funny calling him names, so he's a fag, why the fuck should you care? What's it got to do with you?* He told them to go home *Enough of your bullshit. He came this close to beating them up himself* my mother concluded.

My mother told me another story from my father's life when, around the age of twenty, he had decided to quit the factory, to give up everything and head for the south of France. *He told his boss to go fuck himself, and it wasn't an easy thing to do, you know people around here never go any-where. They go straight from collège to the factory and they spend their whole life in the village or they move a couple of towns over but never too far. But your dad really up and left.*

So my father left. It must have been something he had often dreamed of doing. He imagined that down there the sun would make factory life more bearable, that the women there would be prettier. He left. He tried to find work in Toulon. My mother: *He tried finding work as a barman but I imagine he spent more time at the bar drinking than actually asking for work. I don't know if he maybe traded odd jobs for things, or what really went on, cause your dad isn't exactly talkative, but I know he lived with an old lady. An old lady with lots of money. A Mormon if I remember right.*

During his trip he had become friends with a young troublemaker (my mother said: *a pick-pocketer*; she was always mispronouncing things) who went by the name of *Snow*, an ironic nickname given his dark Maghrebi complexion. They became extremely close, spent all their nights together, and the pair of them would go out to pick up women. For a few months they were inseparable, but then my father came back north, for reasons my mother didn't know. His past caught up with him, as if despite his best efforts there was no way to escape. This was something my mother didn't understand: *So that's why your dad never talks about this stuff, his trip when he lived down south, because it's pretty strange, it don't make sense, when he says we should kill all the ragheads but then when he lived in the Midi his best mate was a raghead. I'm telling you this because I can't figure out why your dad is such a racist, cause I'm not, even if it's true the Arabs and the blacks get away with everything, and the government spends way too much money on them so there's less for us, but still it's not like I'm for killing them or hanging them or putting them in camps like your dad is.*

On why men don't trust doctors

Pressured by my father's insults and remarks, I eventually started hanging out with a couple of boys from the village. If I called them *my mates, the gang,* anyone could have seen that this was pure fantasy, and that I was actually an isolated unit orbiting around them. I never managed to become fully integrated into groups of other boys. There were many parties that I never heard about, football games no one asked me to join, the kinds of things that wouldn't matter to an adult but leave a kid scarred.

A couple of times each week we would meet up in our neighbour's woodshed, with no particular plans in mind. It was a huge shack right in the middle of the back yard, imposing, as if it had been thrown together in a hurry or had survived a terrible storm, and was on the verge of collapse. Something like this existed in nearly everyone's garden, made out of large, thin pieces of sheet metal people got from the dump. In those days – not so long ago, in fact, just at the dawn of the twenty-first century, but the village, far from the city with its movement and activity, was also sheltered from the passage of time – chain-link fences hadn't yet come to divide one yard from another, so we all shared a huge communal space behind the houses which allowed us to meet up easily, without letting the adults know, without being seen by anyone.

We'd spend the afternoon playing amid the woodpiles and the sawdust, evidence of the hours men spent cutting up logs to feed their stoves and heat their houses. I'd walk around barefoot in the midst of rusty nails and pieces of bark covered with fungus, my mother screaming *You don't go walking around barefoot, it's dangerous, there's nails in the wood, you'll get tetanus or an infection. What's going on in your head that you can't put some shoes on and pay attention.* Or: *He may be good at school, but he's still a bit slow, that one.*

One day, just as she had predicted, I stepped on a nail. Out of shame, or pride really, I couldn't let her know she was right. I decided not to tell anyone and to hide the wound in my right foot made by the nail. A few days later an oozing black mark appeared on my foot and seemed to become increasingly serious, growing larger, spreading like a spot of ink on fabric. A few more days passed during which I became consumed with worry, as when a realisation dawns too late and plunges you into inertia. It was one of those cases where the more time passes, the less able you are to correct your mistake or to set right some embarrassing situation, and so it becomes harder and harder to react. I did finally decide – having made a mighty effort to wrench myself into action, to stop merely contemplating this ever more serious, not to say danger-ous, situation – to start disinfecting the wound every day (multiple times a day, in fact, since by now I wasn't just worried, I was panicked by that endlessly resonant word about which I knew nothing, or next to nothing: *tetanus*) with perfume – the cheap, revolting-smelling perfume that my mother wore. When she smelled the perfume on me, she asked me if I'd gone crazy, wearing a woman's perfume, the one my own mother wore. She came up with the hypothesis of madness in order to avoid pro-nouncing that other word, *faggot*, in order not to think about the possibility that I was gay, to push it aside, to convince herself that I'd lost my mind, which would be preferable to having a fairy for a son.

I had inherited from my father this heedlessness where health problems were concerned. In fact, it was more than simply heedlessness, it was mistrust, it was hostility towards doctors and medicine. It would take me years, even after I was grown up, even after I had left the village behind, to accept the idea of taking medicine. Even today, I cannot help feeling a sort of repulsion at the idea of ingesting antibiotics or of calling a doctor. In a more gen-eral way – it wasn't just my father – men didn't like that kind of thing. They made a principle out of it *You won't see me popping pills all the time, I'm no fairy.* I was shaped by this resistance to medicine, especially given my obsessive desire to identify with or to mimic – to ape, you might say – masculine characteristics. 'Someone who does not feel himself to be a man will all the more wish to appear one and someone who knows his own inner weakness is all the more ready to exhibit displays of strength.'

My uncle had paid the price for this masculine neglect. He had smoked his whole life, never worrying about what was excessive, or what was a reasonable limit, never thinking about moderation. His teeth were yellow from tobacco, more black than yellow, his clothes reeked of Gitanes. He had smoked, but also he'd drunk a lot after work, like my father, in order to forget the exhausting days of hauling around cases and crates, of having fifteen minutes in which to eat, with your eye on your watch, the lousy heated-up lunch your wife had prepared the night before and put in your lunch tin. Then there was the noise of the sorting room, deafening, a kind of assault, even. There's barely enough time to sit down for lunch, and if you go a minute over the foreman starts to yell. My mother would tell me about his increasingly pronounced drinking habit *That's how he became an alcoholic, your uncle did, like all the others, they're really all the same, not a single one of them who holds the others back.* More and more often he'd be seen staggering down the street, yelling insults at the other villagers, making obscene remarks to the younger women *Hey baby, bring that pretty arse over here, and let's do it, come on you little slut, you know you want it* going so far as to undo his clothes and expose himself in public. My aunt tried to keep her dignity, pretending not to know about her husband's behaviour, when she saw the other women in front of the school.

In the end, someone found him face down, unconscious, in the street, nearly dead, his face a mess, the skin scraped raw by his fall, and his nose broken. It was an alcohol-induced coma. The person who found him called the paramedics.

My uncle found face down on the asphalt, my uncle taken to the hospital in an ambulance. Within a few minutes at least half the village had gathered around his motionless body. My aunt came to see us that same evening, her face hard and impassive, her eyes dry. She told us it was bad. My uncle had smoked too much, drunk too much, his appallingly unhealthy way of life had led to a stroke. He was paralysed *The doctor said to me that maybe he won't even wake up, but I always told him to stop drinking, I told him but he didn't listen to a word I said. Too damn foolish, that's what he was.*

Two weeks later I learned that there was a word *hemiplegia* and what it meant. The entire left side of my uncle's body was paralysed. He would be bedridden for the rest of his life – and, as the doctor specified with the sad look on his face that doctors have under these circumstances – he didn't have much time left. His condition got worse and worse. Coughing fits would last for hours, he'd cry out all day, and even more at night, when he would wake my aunt to have her change his position, turn him another way because his limbs had fallen asleep, *pins and needles in my arms*. My aunt: *I've had it, I'm about ready to kill myself, I can't take it any more.* There were his fits of dementia, most likely brought on by the situation, by the boredom of being bedridden in his own front room. There wasn't enough room in the bedroom to install the *hospital bed* there. He would insult my aunt *Bitch, you can't wait for me to die, it's all you dream of.*

My aunt: *And when he says that to me it's not fair, cause if I wanted to I could've had him sent to a home, I could've and I didn't, I wanted to be with him and take care of him, and I'll take care of him till he dies, after all, I'm his wife.*

Despite everything my uncle refused to take care of himself.

My aunt, again: *And there's nothing I can say to him, he's got his pride, he never liked pills and he's a man there's nothing I can say. So tough luck for him because if he goes on like that there's things that could happen to him, just like what happened to Sylvain.*

Sylvain (an eyewitness account)

Sylvain was very much admired in my family. My cousin Sylvain, ten years older than me, a real tough guy, had spent much of his youth stealing mopeds, organising break-ins where he stole·televisions and game consoles in order to resell them later, vandalising public buildings, blowing up mailboxes. He had several arrests for dealing drugs or driving drunk with his kids in the back seat *He was getting into trouble. He wasn't like you, he couldn't stand school.* Whenever my aunt or any other relative spoke of Sylvain's exploits, any worry or disapproval they felt was always outweighed by their pride at having such a truly tough guy in the family *Sylvain better cool it a bit or he'll lose custody of those kids.*

Sylvain had been raised by our grandmother after his mother lost custody of her children because, I think, of her alcoholism. She had already come to the attention of family services because she had had most of her children with her own cousin.

After a series of petty convictions of various kinds, and because he was always getting into the same kind of trouble, the court made the decision – for months already the sentence had been hanging over his head – to send him to prison for eight months. My grandmother would come back from visiting him and tell us about all the difficulties he was having: fights with the other inmates, daily life in prison, which was especially hard on the poorest inmates. Everything there had to be paid for *Can you believe he even has to pay for toilet paper. It's disgraceful.* And also there was something my grandmother couldn't really bring herself to say, something she could only insinuate and that made her blush and lower her eyes, which was that some inmates raped other ones – like, as it turned out, Sylvain. She wasn't totally certain about this because Sylvain would barely let out a word on the subject, just like her. A humiliation shared without words.

After he'd spent a few weeks in prison, the court allowed him a weekend's release, long enough to see his family and friends, *for good behaviour,* my grandmother said. He had planned a schedule down to the minute, he'd spent hours, whole nights dreaming about it in his bunk, organising his days of freedom like an excited child as the weekend got closer and closer and the schedule he was planning became more and more concrete (here I am simply trying to imagine, to reconstitute what must have been my cousin's state of mind at that moment). He had told my grandmother how happy he felt during his leave. He realised that someone who had gone through so many difficulties was better able to experience happiness than anyone else. He had understood that one existed only in relation to the other and that people who had always lived comfortably, who had never known want or humiliation were missing out. As if they'd never really lived.

He had been able to make love to his wife, play with his children, choose when and what to eat. *He went to McDonald's pretty damn quick, he'd been missing it.*

My grandmother told us the rest of the story looking miserable as she did so.

When he came to see me – it was at night the day before he was supposed to go back to his prison cell – I saw it right away. I could see it in his eyes, that something was bothering him, because I know my Sylvain well, I'm the one that brought him up. I've learned. He looked sad, but then, at the same time, I don't really know how to say it, it's hard to explain, he also looked pleased, because he knew he wasn't going back. He'd already made up his mind. You know I even think that the second he opened the door and walked in, that very second, in the blink of an eye, I knew he had made up his mind never to set foot in that place again. What was I supposed to say, tell me, it'd been a long time since I'd seen him anywhere near to as happy as he was then, my Sylvain, and it would've done no good, you know how he is. No one has ever made him change his mind.

He's tough.

At first, he sat down and acted like there was nothing going on. He asked me, and he never did this, he never did this in nearly thirty years, so that was just one more clue, he asked me what I'd been up to that day. What a stupid question. It was dumb because he already knew. But I played along. I told him: I went to get some bread at the bakery, I fed the chickens, and then I just watched TV on the sofa. Just like usual. There he sat, like a piece of furniture. Then there was this long silence. You know those kinds of moments, when the silence seems to last for ever. It's almost like you start counting the seconds and each one lasts an hour. It makes you nervous. I mean, usually, around Sylvain, I'm not nervous. Ever. I'm the one who raised him, so when there's a silence, a minute later you forget about it. It doesn't mean anything, that's how life is. It's not even that you don't care, you don't even notice. But that day, that day was different.

At the end of that long silence, my cousin spoke. What made it so hard was that he knew my grandmother had understood. She'd already guessed what he was about to say. And what if he said it wrong, so that she didn't understand him? The point wasn't to reveal something to her, but to make sure she would accept what she already knew. So he simply declared that he wasn't going back to prison. He didn't say that he didn't want to, as if it were a question of will, as if there were a choice to be made, but simply that he couldn't, it just wasn't possible. He couldn't go on eating that same food day after day *I swear Gran, people always go on about what they feed you in hospitals, but in there it's even worse.* To have to see the inmates he hated, or even the friends he had made there, the ones he hung out with during breaks in the yard, the ones he spoke to about his wife and kids, the ones who had become a second family for him, the ones he called *my clan*, the ones who protected him, helped him, and whom he protected and helped in return, he hated them too, if he thought about it (as if others, individual people, were always associated with a place, a space, a particular time, from which they could never be disassociated, as if there were a geography to bonds, to friendships, and hating a particular place would inevitably, inexorably imply hating the people who were found there). He couldn't bear the stink of the cellblock, or the sound of the crazy guy upstairs who beat his fists against the wall every night, rattling not the metal bars, because those hardly exist in modern prisons, but the metal doors that have replaced them. Sylvain was upset less by the noise the crazy guy would make than by the fear that someday that could be him, that someday he would be the one who, worn out from being locked up in that tiny space for so long, would tip over into madness.

My grandmother: *So he told me, Gran I'm really sorry but I won't be going back there. He looked me straight in the eyes.*

And I didn't look away. I looked right back at him to show him
that what he was saying was something I could understand okay,
I wasn't shocked. He didn't need to choose nice words to talk to
me. Don't matter that I'm a woman. So what did I do? I made
a face to make it look like I was thinking it over, or a little angry,
so I could be sure if his mind was really made up about what
he wanted to do. He knew what I was doing. Suppose I'd have
said no, that he had to go back, he would've told me, and really
he wouldn't have been totally wrong, he would've said: You want
me to die in jail, you want me to croak in there? I couldn't let
myself do that. I asked him

Your mind's made up, are you sure? He replied: Yes Gran
cause if I go back there you'll never see me again, that's for sure.
I was pretty shook up when he said that. I was trying not to cry
and I'm not the kind of woman who cries easily. I pretended to
blow my nose saying it's the damn hay they're cutting that gives
me allergies. He gave me a kiss and then he left.

Sylvain went home after that. He celebrated his freedom
with a few friends. For a while, everything was fine; the
police didn't come looking for him right away. He must
have imagined, given all the television series he watched,
at least for a moment, that the police would arrive in a
dozen cars and maybe even a helicopter, that they would
surround the house and declare through a megaphone
Mr Bellegueule, we have the house surrounded and you are
under arrest.

When he had got really drunk (*I'm doing some serious drinking tonight to mark the occasion*), he went to find his kids, who were in their bedroom watching a video *Come on kids we're going for a drive*. My father was the same: as soon as he was drunk he had to get behind the wheel. He dared himself to do it. The kids were thrilled; they didn't think to ask why now, why at this hour of the night. They just went to put their shoes on, still in their pyjamas. His wife said *No way*. She told him he'd had too much to drink, and done too many drugs for the night, and that he wasn't thinking straight *You don't really want to go out and smash yourself up and smash the kids up with you*. They got into a fight. Sylvain told his wife she shouldn't be saying things like that. She should know better. She didn't know what he'd been through in prison, what he'd had to put up with, that no matter how hard she tried, she'd never be able to imagine what it had been like. Words he could only have said drunk came out, the kind of things where you never know if they've been lurking deep inside of the person who says them, or if there's no truth to them at all *And anyway it's your own fault that I ended up in jail, cause you didn't know how to love me, if you had I wouldn't have needed to do all the shit I did, I was just trying to make up for the love no one ever gave me, starting with my mother who left me, in fact everyone has always left me if you stop to think about it*. The kinds of things talk-show psychologists would say, which my grandmother had put into his head. She had already told me that Sylvain's wife didn't know how to take care of him and that this made her in some way responsible for his behaviour. In the village responsibility for men's behaviour was frequently assigned to women, whose duty it was to keep them under control, as, for instance, during the fights at the end of evening dances *As for that wife of his, she didn't give a fuck about him. A real bitch.*

After their argument, Sylvain took the car and left without the kids, anger agitating every fibre in his body. A few kilometres down the road, he was stopped by the police.

My grandmother again: *Yeah well of course the police knew what was up when they pulled him over. It was all a set up. They didn't say anything right away, they pretended it was a routine stop, something unrelated. Pretending they didn't know who he was. Asking him to breathe into the breathalyser, and when he did, they must have been relieved, cause now they had another pretext for arresting him. It wouldn't have mattered, they would have done it anyway, but now they had an extra reason, aggravating circumstances they call it. Then because he was really living it up he had smoked some weed, and cops aren't idiots, they're used to this, it's their job after all. They could smell it right away. They did a blood alcohol test and you know Sylvain, he could throw them back. He could drink anyone under the table. Now I can't really know for sure, but I bet the cops were taking their time and letting him sit there and stew, telling themselves he'd just get more scared if they made him wait. The one who was doing the talking, I think it was the chief, asked Sylvain for his licence and registration and then went back to his squad car to do a computer check, on that little computer they have in all the cop cars now so that they can recognise people right away. Identify them.*

Then Sylvain just freaked out. He just pressed the accelerator down all the way like he was going to escape. So what did the cop do? He jumped right in front of the car, I guess to stop him from running off. I've got no idea what went through Sylvain's head, something snapped, he went crazy like dogs can sometimes do when usually they're gentle as can be and then one day they attack the little girl who's just sitting there quietly playing with her dolls in the living room, and they rip her face off and either the girl's dead or her face is deformed for the rest of her life, and often enough in cases like that the dog knows the little girl really well, it's the family dog, and they've spent hours and hours together, and the little mutt was the nicest thing in the world. And then the parents are trying to get the dog to calm down but in cases like that you can try whatever you want, there's nothing you can do, not a thing. Can you imagine that, the dog you raised, the dog you fed, the dog you petted over and over again, you see it right there in front of you and then one fine day with no warning at all, there it is trying to eat your kids. You throw yourself on the dog, you hit it as hard as you can, I hear that when you are really angry or really afraid you are way stronger, ten times stronger, you shout, you cry, anyway, I'm just trying to imagine something that's never happened to me thank goodness.

But the more you hit the dog, the more it sinks its teeth into your little girl's neck, and there's blood all over the room, it's squirting everywhere, and your little girl is trying to scream but she can't, you can just hear some air coming out of her mouth, I think you call that a rattle, and so then, what do I know, I'm just trying to imagine it, so then you run to the kitchen to find a butcher's knife and you come back and stab the damn mutt. It might seem easy to kill someone like that, but really, I know this from when I kill my chickens to cook them, really it's hard. You really have to press on the knife so that it goes deep into the flesh, you have to be strong. You have to want to do it, let me tell you. And there you are stabbing the dog over and over but it's too late, cause when you've finally managed to kill the damn thing, you realise your little girl's half dead too. That's two dead bodies to deal with.

Anyway that's not what I was trying to say to you, that's not what I wanted to say. Sylvain. He presses down on the accelerator, the cop gets in front of the car to stop him from driving off, but something snaps in Sylvain's head and he takes off, he accelerates heading straight for the policeman and he hits him. The cop flies up over the windscreen. It's okay, he's not seriously hurt, he gets straight up and he and his colleagues begin to chase Sylvain, just like the chase scenes you see on TV. But my little man knows how to handle himself, so he gets away. He loses them.

They found Sylvain a few hours later at a construction site for a new housing estate. He knew he would be arrested in the end. He went out to the site with a baseball bat that he always had in his car in case one of the boys to whom he owed money – drug-dealing – snuck up on him and attacked him to get his money back. He had broken all the windows one by one, his cries resonating in the still night air. He had broken them all, tried to set things on fire, yelling louder and louder, so that you might have believed he was trying to let the neighbours (and through them the police) know he was there. He didn't want to go to jail, to be sent back inside, just because he'd failed to respect the terms of his leave. He wanted to do something to really deserve it. When the police arrived, they found him surrounded by shards of glass and pieces of the bricks and tiles that he had thrown against the walls. He had spray painted *FTP* in giant letters on the wall. He didn't resist when they put the handcuffs on him.

Sylvain appeared in front of the judge. He looked very calm, just as when the police had arrested him. Less agitated than one might have thought and than he might have been before. The prosecutor asked him the usual questions: why he had done it, why in that exact way, questions about his past, his children, his private life *As for your father whom you never knew and your mother who abandoned you, do you think that all of that, that all those details from your past had anything to do with your delinquent behaviour?* There were other questions he couldn't understand because of the language used, not just the legal language, but the language of individuals who had some education *Can you affirm that your acts are imputable to external influences of some kind or is it your feeling that you were in full control of yourself during this incident?* My cousin stammered that he hadn't understood the question and he asked for it to be repeated. He wasn't embarrassed, he didn't feel the violence the prosecutor was exercising, the class violence that had excluded him from the world of education, the violence that had, in the end, led him to the courtroom where he now stood. In fact he must have thought that the prosecutor was ridiculous. That he spoke like a faggot.

The final question in the series the prosecutor asked him was – and this was a mere formality since everyone was sure they knew – what he had meant to say with *FTP*. My family had been discussing it ever since the arrest *You know it's true he could never stand the cops, he really just hated the sight of them.* The prosecutor asked him why he hated the police so much, why he had made a point of going to his car for a can of spray paint while he was in the middle of ransacking the construction site (fragments of glass, brick, and slate), so that he could spray *FTP*, which, as everyone could tell, meant *Fuck the Police*, on the wall, since that was an act that required premeditation and – consequently – didn't seem consistent with the deranged state suggested by Sylvain's behaviour at the construction site. *But Mr Prosecutor, sir, you've got it all wrong. FTP doesn't stand for Fuck the Police. It stands for Fuck the Prosecutor.* That affront to the prosecutor's dignity still makes people in my family shudder when they tell the story *He really had balls, that one.* He went back to jail with a sentence of six years. Then he was diagnosed with advanced lung cancer. He refused treatment. He was found dead in his prison cell one morning. He wasn't even thirty years old.

(I went back to spend two days in the village where I grew up to gather some information about my family. My plan was to see my grandmother and to ask her questions about Sylvain. I met with her in her new home in a little low-income housing development, where all the houses are exactly alike. She had moved out of the house she had always lived in and sold it to my sister. This was only the second time I had visited her in the new place. The first time I visited, it was clean, but this time I had the sense that my grandmother was slowly taking the place over. It smelled filthy; it smelled of filthy dogs – and she did have a small dog with her in her house of thirty square metres, whereas all the dogs from her old house had since died. I don't quite know how to describe this odour of filthy dogs, but you often smell it around town, including at my mother's house. She offered me something to drink and I said yes. She gave me a dirty glass. I remained silent. I didn't dare say anything. I took the glass into which she poured a little strawberry syrup. Then she went back to the kitchen where she rinsed out an empty bottle of detergent and then filled it up with water. I realised she was going to use it as a pitcher. I tried not to let my disgust show, and said nothing when she poured a little of the water into my glass, horrified by the flakes of detergent that were in it. For two hours I asked her questions about our family, but never took a sip. She kept throwing furtive and questioning glances towards my glass.)

Two

Failure and Flight

The shed

This happened not long after the two boys first hit me. A few months later at the most.

It all began on one of those days we spent in our neighbour's woodshed. That afternoon Bruno had suggested we all go to his house: his parents weren't home. He suggested we go into his room and watch a film; he was quite insistent *You've got to see this, it's something else.* We did whatever he said because we were five or six years younger than him, and he had us call him *the boss*.

He told us to sit on his bed, on a mattress that had been white once, or off-white, but was now brown and orange with dirt, producing clouds of dust when we sat down, and a shut-in kind of smell, like a damp cupboard. He disappeared for a few seconds. When he came back he had a video cassette in his hand, a pornographic film *A porn film I stole from my dad, he doesn't know it, cause if he did he'd kill me for sure.* He suggested we watch it together. The other two, my cousin Stéphane and Fabien, Bruno's other neighbour, agreed. I, on the other hand, didn't want to. I said it was impossible, we couldn't do that. I added that it seemed weird to me, and even kind of perverted, for guys to watch a porn film together. My cousin then made a suggestion as if he were amused by it, in a voice just playful enough that if we reacted badly, he could claim to have been joking, that his suggestion had been meant as a joke, that he would never seriously have gone through with it, but also with just enough seriousness and authority in his tone that we would understand that he actually meant it, suggesting that we all masturbate together while we watched the film. There was a moment of silence. Everyone was observing everyone else trying to figure out how to react. No one wanted to risk giving an answer that set them apart, or made the others laugh at them.

I don't remember who risked it first and accepted my cousin's offer, which led to general agreement. But I couldn't accept *I really don't want to see your guys' dicks, I'm not a fucking faggot.*

I stayed away from anything that seemed even a little bit gay. One night, we were at the recreation ground – in those days, before the renovations that would come later, it was really little more than a large expanse of green grass with a few rusty goal posts rising up out of it – where we'd climb over the fence to get into it at night when we weren't supposed to be there. We'd go there from the bus stop to drink our beers. On that night, my cousin Stéphane, who had been drinking, began to say crazy things about himself and about how strong he was *I'm a monster, you guys, a beast, I'll kill anyone who touches me.* Then he took off all his clothes, piece by piece, in order to show off the powerful physique he was talking about, until finally he was totally naked. In the village, men would do this with some regularity when they were drunk, my paralysed uncle was one example before his accident, or Arnaud and Jean, who would end up totally naked at the end of the annual village party, standing on top of the row of tables that had been assembled so that the villagers could socialise together around platters of chips and grilled sausages. The grilling had been done by Fabien's father, *Merguez*, who got his nickname because he took charge of the grilling during the village celebrations and at the flea markets. Fabien also got called *Merguez*: nicknames were hereditary.

The others were all laughing *He is so shit-faced, he's feeling no pain, barking at the fucking moon.* My cousin was running from one end of the field to the other, naked, showing off his penis, whose remarkable size made me uncomfortable. Then the other boys, laughing wildly, joined the game and started getting undressed. They were all running around, playing with themselves and with the other boys. Their penises would flop back and forth from one thigh to the other along with the movements of their bodies, slapping against one leg, then the other, then their bellies. They would rub up against each other, skin to skin, as if they were having sex. Boys enjoy laughing about things like that.

One of them asked me why I didn't join in. I answered in a voice loud enough to be heard by all of them that I wasn't into these sorts of games, and once again, as with the film that Bruno had found, I said this kind of thing *makes me want to puke*, and that as I looked at them, in the state they were in, all naked, I couldn't help thinking they were behaving like a bunch of fags. The truth was that the display of all these bits of flesh was driving me a little crazy. I was using words like *fags, fairies, queers* to keep my distance from them. I used these words against the others in the hope that they would stop invading every inch of my own body.

I remained seated on the ground, disapproving of their behaviour. Pretending to be gay was their way of showing that they really weren't. You would really have to not be a fag to be able to spend an evening pretending to be one without running the risk of attracting insults.

What I thought didn't matter much. Decisions were, as was always and everywhere the case, the prerogative of men, and I wasn't one of them. The decision had to be made by Bruno and the others. I don't remember if they

told me to be quiet or if that process of silencing func-
tioned without anyone really noticing it. They hadn't
listened to me and they put the cassette into the VCR.
When the first images appeared they joked around a little, but then the agitation slowly began to shift in nature.
Their breathing became more and more halting. Bodies
sweaty, eyes glued to the screen, eagerness perceptible on
everyone's lips, which trembled slightly, especially at the
corners of their mouths. They unzipped their trousers
and started playing with themselves. I can still hear the
moans, real moans of pleasure. I can still see the dampness
on their cocks.

I said I had to leave and that I didn't want to be part
of this game, it was too messed up. I didn't say that I was
unsettled; I tried to keep that hidden, to display com-
posure. When I got home I broke down in tears, torn
between the desire the other boys had provoked in me
and the disgust I felt towards myself, towards my own
desiring body.

I went back and spent time with them as soon as the next
day. We didn't talk about the film right away.

We got together in the shed just like on the other days,
to make wooden weapons by carving up the logs that
were there. On this particular day, my cousin interrupted
the noise of the saws and the hammers *Damn that was
hot, that film we watched, fucking hot* (my heart is beating so
loudly as he says these words that I have the impression

that each heartbeat could be fatal, that my heart won't be able to tolerate such beating much longer). He continued *Too fucking bad that we can't do the same things the actors were doing.* He waited for a few seconds then went back to work (on his log), before adding *In any case we don't have enough girls to do it, and the girls around here are too uptight anyway* (sound of a hammer, then a heartbeat, sound of a hammer, then a heartbeat; the two together combine in an infernal symphony).

When, shortly after that, he asked the question, it came almost out of nowhere. My mother would have said *It just appeared, like when all of a sudden you need to piss.* My cousin suggested *We could try the same things they do in the film.* The reactions were less reticent than one might have expected from kids who, according to their own words, and already when they were only ten years old, when they were too young ever to have seen many, or even one, hated all fags. *Man, that would be totally wild, that would be awesome.* Bruno asked where we could play these games, where we could *do it,* and then suggested we just stay there in the shed. The smiles they fixed on their faces remained as a kind of insurance that they could at any moment turn this delicate plan into a huge joke. They spoke in hushed tones, as if their words were bombs that had to be handled with extreme caution and that could, if they raised their voices, destroy them in a second. My cousin kept reassuring himself and us: it was only a game we were going to play, one afternoon only *We can just do it you know, for fun.* He suggested that I go steal some jewellery from my older sister *Eddy go on, it'll make it even better, it'll make it more, you know, you could steal some rings from your sister, and that way, the person who puts on the ring can be the one who plays the woman, who gets fucked, just for messing around, because like without the rings we might get mixed up, it'll make it more realistic. With the rings we'll know who's who.*

I did as I was told. I didn't know how to refuse. I couldn't manage to pretend any longer that I was unwilling or disgusted. My body left me no choice but to do whatever they might ask. I ran off to my bedroom to pilfer the rings my sister kept hidden in a little purple jewellery box. When I returned, they were still there in the shed and I said *Got em. Show me* Bruno commanded. He gave one to me and one to Fabien. *You two will play the women and me and Stéphane will play the men.* They didn't seem nervous any more. It was more like they were ready to try out a new kind of game, a naughty one, but still just a game kids play, like the days on which Bruno would amuse himself by torturing his mother's chickens. I remember chickens hanged with fishing line, chickens letting out indescribable, inimitable cries of horror, chickens burned alive, and even one chicken that spent a football match serving as a ball. I realised that I was being propelled into this situation by everything I was made of, by all the desire that had been repressed for so long. I was burning with excitement.

I lay face down on the ground, or more exactly, face down in the sawdust that carpeted the floor of the shed and that got sucked into my mouth each time I took a breath. My cousin pulled down my trousers and handed me one of the rings I had brought *Hey put the ring on, or else it's no good.*

I felt his penis hard against my buttocks and then inside me. He gave me directions *Spread them, lift your arse a little.* I obeyed his orders with the sense that I was in the process of turning into what I had always been. At every thrust he made, I got a little harder, and just like when they watched the film for the first time, the giggles that they made during the first few thrusting motions quickly changed into imitations of the moans of the porn actors, and their lines that just then seemed like the most beautiful words I had ever heard *Take it, take my cock, you know you like it.* At the same time as my cousin was taking possession of my body, Bruno was doing the same to Fabien, just a few centimetres away. I was breathing in the smell of naked bodies and wishing I could turn that smell into a substance so that I could eat it, and make it more real. I wanted it to be a poison that could intoxicate me and make me disappear, with my last memory being the smell of those bodies, ones that already bore the marks of their social class, where beneath the smooth, milky skin of children, adult muscles were starting to form, already developed because of the time spent helping their fathers chop and stack wood, because of all the physical activity, the endless football games played day after day. Bruno was older than us, fifteen at that time whereas we were only nine or ten, so his penis was massive in comparison to ours and surrounded by brown hair. He already had a man's body. As I watched him penetrating Fabien I was overtaken with jealousy. I dreamed of killing Fabien and my cousin Stéphane so that I could have Bruno's body all to myself, his strong arms, his legs with their bulging muscles. I even dreamed of Bruno being dead so that he could never, ever get away from me, so that his body would always be mine.

This was the first in a whole series of afternoons where we would get together to re-enact scenes from the film and then scenes from other films we managed to see. We had to be careful not to be caught by our mothers, who would come out into the back yard a few times a day to pull up weeds in the garden, dig up a few vegetables, or get wood from the shed. When one of them approached, somehow we found the time to pull our clothes back on and to pretend to be playing at something else.

We worked ourselves into a kind of frenzy. Not a day would go by when I wouldn't meet up with Bruno, or my cousin Stéphane, or Fabien, and now not only in the shed but in any likely place, in order, as we would say *to play man and woman*, behind the trees at the back of the yard, in Bruno's attic, in the streets. Once my hands had taken on the smell of their genitals, I wouldn't wash them; I'd spend hours sniffing at them, like an animal. They smelled like what I was.

During this period, the idea that I really was a girl in a boy's body, as everyone had always told me, came to seem more and more real. Little by little I had become an invert. I was swimming in confusion. Meeting with the boys every day in the shed in order to undress them, to penetrate them or be penetrated by them, encouraged me to say to myself that some kind of an error had occurred – I knew that mistakes like this could be made. I had always heard, from all quarters, that girls liked boys. So if I liked boys, then surely I was a girl. I dreamed of my body changing, of one day being surprised to notice that my penis had disappeared. I imagined it fading away during the night and being replaced by a girl's sex the next morning. I never saw a shooting star without wishing that I'd stop being a boy. There was not a single page of my journal on which I didn't make some reference to my secret desire to become a girl – and then the fear, which was always present, that my mother would discover this journal.

Then one day it all ended.

It was my mother. She had no way of knowing that she would indirectly contribute to the multiplication of insults at school, to the beatings. I was in the shed with the three others. Stéphane was lying on top of me, and I was wearing the sign of femininity, the ring on my index finger. Bruno was penetrating Fabien. My mother appeared. We hadn't seen her approach, but she was there carrying a glass dish filled with grain to feed the poultry. When I discovered her there, in front of us – too late to notice the moment of rupture, the second in which she had been obliged to change from a woman feeding her chickens, a task that was part of the daily routine, into a mother who is watching her son, just ten years old, being sodomised by his own cousin, and she shared my father's opinions about homosexuality, even if she expressed them less frequently – when I noticed her she was already standing frozen, unable to make the slightest sound or the smallest gesture. She was staring at me in the way one might imagine in a situation like this, a perfectly common one really, the situation of a person who, with no warning, stumbles across a scene so unthinkable that she stands there unable to react, jaw hanging open, eyes popping out of their sockets.

For several seconds neither one of us was able to do anything at all. Then she dropped the glass dish, which broke against a pile of logs. She didn't look at it, didn't lower her eyes towards the dish, the way you do when something breaks. Her gaze never left mine; I don't remember what that gaze held. Disgust perhaps, or anguish – I can no longer say. I was too blinded by my own shame and by the idea that suddenly popped into my head that she might tell everyone everything, my father, his mates, the women in the village whose voices I could already hear *Everyone always said he was a little off, the Bellegueule kid, that he wasn't like the others, what with all those gestures he'd make when he'd be talking, that kind of stuff, everyone knew there was a little bit of a fag in him.*

My mother left without saying a word. I got dressed quickly. I wanted to get home as fast as I could, desperate to keep her from saying anything to anyone else. To beg her if I had to.

It was already too late.

When I opened the door my mother was there. She had the same frozen expression on her face as five minutes before, as if it would be paralysed for the rest of her life, as if the shock had disfigured her for ever. My father was standing next to her, wearing a similar expression. He knew everything. He walked up to me slowly, then came the blow, a powerful slap across my face, with his other hand gripping my T-shirt so hard that it ripped, another slap, a third, and then another and another, with not a word being said. Suddenly *Don't you ever do that again. You ever do that again and things will go really bad for you.*

After the shed

For the next few weeks I didn't hear any more about what had happened in the shed. I hoped it was just going to be forgotten. And yet the omnipresence of it felt crushing: every time my parents looked at me it was a warning, everything about their tone of voice, every one of their gestures told me to keep quiet. It was not to be mentioned. No one was to be told what had happened, ever; to talk about it would be a way of making it happen again.

So when it did suddenly reappear, it wasn't as if it had left me. Still I wasn't expecting it. I assumed the shame we all shared, me, my parents, and my *mates*, was too power-ful, that it would prevent any one of us from mentioning it and so protect me. I was wrong.

The two boys came up to me in the corridor. It wasn't exactly every morning that they did this. Some days they didn't show up: they were frequently absent from school, like me and everybody else, they'd use any excuse to skip school. Other times, I would be so scared and really so tired of this endless game, as if it had always been nothing more than a game, that I didn't want to take part any more. Not to go to that hallway, not to wait for them there, not to get beaten up, the same way some people will just give up everything, family, friends, work, and decide that the life they've been leading no longer makes any sense, no longer believing in a life that was only being held together by belief. And yet I kept on going back to the library despite everything, despite the fear of seeing them turn up, and my anxiety over what kinds of retaliation the next day might bring.

They seemed especially worked up. I had learned to read the expressions on their faces. After two years of being together in this hallway on a daily basis, I knew them better than anyone else. I could tell on which days they were tired, on which days less so. I swear that there were times when one of them seemed sad, and I would feel sorry for him, worried about him. I would spend the day wondering, trying to figure out what might be wrong. When they spat in my face, I could have told you what they'd been eating. By now I knew them really well.

They smiled and wanted to know if it was true, the new rumour that was going round. The thing everyone was talking about, the main subject of conversation of all the kids at the school. They wanted to know — and they almost didn't believe it, it was too good to be true, exactly what they'd always hoped for — if in fact my cousin, yes, my own cousin, had done to me what he said he had. *It's your cousin who snitched on you, he told everyone.* He said that one afternoon in the shed, when he went off in a corner to urinate, I went over to him and rubbed his penis with my fingertips. In his version, as told to me by the two boys, I pulled down my trousers too, and rubbed up against him, and then I got down on my knees and took his penis in my mouth. He had told everyone that after that he had *buttfucked* me, that I had liked it and moaned *just like a girl* and that I had *even brought along a ring to pretend to be a girl.*

The tall redhead grabbed my throat to make me answer right away. His cold fingers on the back of my neck, the smile on my face, fear, the confession that was expected. *My cousin's making shit up. He's a little weird, that's why they put him in all those remedial classes with the special needs kids at school. I'm no fucking sissy.* I wasn't fooling anyone. Nothing would have put them off, in any case, even if the whole story had been untrue. My cousin's story fitted the image they had of me too well. He got annoyed *Stop lying you fucking poof we know it's true.*

He didn't spit in my face. That morning, he spat on the sleeve of my jacket, a greenish gob so thick it just sat there. The short one with the hunched back did the same thing, on the same sleeve (a thin blue running jacket with black stripes that I wore in winter; I had lost my coat and my parents weren't able to buy me a new one *Sort it out yourself, it's your fault for losing it*). They laughed. I looked at the gobs of spit stuck on my jacket, thinking at least they had spared me by spitting there and not in my face. And then the tall redhead said to me *Eat the spit faggot*. I smiled, again, just like I always did. Not that I thought they were joking, but I hoped, by smiling, to shift the situation and turn it into a joke. He repeated *Eat the spit faggot, and hurry up about it*. I refused – normally I didn't, I almost never refused, but I didn't want to eat the gobs of spit; it would have made me vomit. I said I didn't want to. One of them grabbed my arm and the other grabbed my head. They forced my face down on to the spittle, ordering me to *Lick it, faggot, lick it*. I slowly stuck my tongue out and licked their spit, whose odour took over my mouth. With each lick of my tongue they would encourage me in a soft, paternal voice (hands gripping my head) *That's it, like that, go on, that's it*. I continued licking the jacket while they went on giving their orders, until the gobs had disappeared. Then they left.

From that day forward, the first waking minutes of every day became more and more unreal. I woke up feeling drunk. The rumour had spread and at school I got looked at more and more. I would hear *faggot* more frequently in the hallways, and find little notes in my book bag *Die you queer*. In the village, where till now I had mostly been spared by the grown-ups, insults cropped up for the first time.

There was one summer's evening when I was playing football with a few other boys in the middle of the street: sweaty T-shirts and an air thick with tension as in all the improvised matches where we'd mark out an imaginary playing field by laying our rucksacks and sweaters on the ground. I was on a team with Stéphane and a few others.

Fabien, Kevin, Steven and Jordan, my *mates*, would get annoyed by my incompetence and would lash out at the first opportunity. *Are you fucking trying to make us lose, you can't play worth shit. Next time no way are you on our team.* I wasn't the only person to whom those kinds of things would be said. Being irritated and cursing were part of the game.

On this evening, however, which was a few weeks after Stéphane had told everyone what had happened, albeit reinventing certain key parts of it, things went differently. One of them said the kind of thing you wish you could forget, and then forget forgetting so that it would disappear entirely – that I'd be better off spending time playing football than screwing my cousin. *You should spend more time on football and less getting your arse fucked by Stéphane.* Even my cousin laughed at this, which mystified me. Why had Stéphane told everyone this story? Why hadn't he felt ashamed or been afraid of being made fun of? Why, on this particular evening when we were all playing football together, but also on all the other evenings when these same insults would resurface, why were none of the insults, none of the hatred, directed at him?

There had been two of us, four really, including Bruno and Fabien. But no one ever mentioned that they'd been in the woodshed, too. There was nothing I could say, for fear of the consequences, and in any case, I knew that informing on them would have done no good, that they would have been spared, just like Stéphane. Logically speaking, he should have been called a *faggot* too. But the crime was not having done something, it was being something. And especially, *looking like* one of them.

Becoming

I remember less the smell of the rapeseed fields than I do the burnt smell that would pervade the village streets when the farmers let manure slowly dry up in the sun. I would cough a lot due to my asthma. A layer of something formed at the back of my throat and on my palate, as if the manure that had evaporated somehow condensed inside my mouth, covering it with a thin grey film.

I remember less the milk still warm from the cow's udders, brought by my mother from the farm across the way than I do the evenings when we didn't have enough to eat, and when my mother would say *Tonight we're having milk*, one of poverty's neologisms.

I don't think the others – my brothers and sisters, my *mates* – suffered as much from village life. But for me, because I couldn't be one of them, I had to reject that whole world. The smoke was unbreathable because of the beatings; the hunger was unbearable because of my father's hatred.

*

I had to get away.

But early on it doesn't occur to you to get away, because you don't know that there's anywhere out there to escape to. You don't even understand that flight is an option. For a while you try to be like others around you, and so I tried to be like everyone else.

When I was twelve those two boys left the school. The tall redhead began studying for a vocational certificate as a painter, and the short one with the hunchback dropped out. He had waited until he was sixteen so his parents wouldn't lose their family benefits. Their departure was a new beginning for me. People still insulted me and made fun of me, but life at school changed completely the day the two of them were no longer around (a new obsession: not to go to the local lycée, not to meet up with them again there).

It seemed necessary that I stop behaving the way I was behaving, the way I had always behaved. I would have to watch the gestures I made while talking, I'd have to make my voice sound deeper, to devote myself exclusively to masculine activities. More football, different television programmes, listen to different CDs. Every morning in the bathroom getting ready I would repeat the same phrase to myself over and over again so many times that it ceased making any sense, becoming nothing but a series of syllables, of sounds. Then I'd stop and start over again *Today I'm gonna be a tough guy.* I remember it because I would always repeat exactly the same sentence, in the same way as you repeat a prayer, in the same words, the exact same words *Today I'm gonna be a tough guy* (and now I'm crying as I write these lines; I'm crying because I find that sentence hideous and ridiculous, that sentence that went everywhere with me for several years and was, I don't think I'm exaggerating, at the centre of my being).

Each day was a new ordeal: people don't change as easily as that. I wasn't the tough guy that I wanted to be. And yet I had understood that living a lie was the only chance I had of bringing a new truth into existence. Becoming a different person meant thinking of myself as a different person, believing I was something I wasn't so that gradually, step by step, I could become it (the calls to conform would come later *Who does he think he is?*).

Laura

Becoming a boy necessarily involved girls. I had met Laura in the same year that the two boys left the school. She had just moved in with a foster family in a neighbouring village. Her mother had decided to give her up. I don't know if there was a specific reason for this. Maybe she was tired of being a mother, the way mine was. Maybe she was so tired of it she couldn't go on. Laura simply told me *My mum doesn't want me any more, I wish I could live with her but she says no.*

Laura had a bad reputation at school. She was one of those city girls – because she and her mother had lived there when she was young – who show up in the village and provoke hostile reactions because of the way they talk, their lifestyle, the way they dress, all of which people in the countryside find shocking. There were the women waiting in front of the school: *A young girl shouldn't be dressing like that at her age, it's disrespectful,* then the school kids: *Laura's a slut.* These rejections made her feel more approachable to me. I had chosen her in order to complete my metamorphosis.

I first approached her through an emissary, one of her closest friends, who lived near me. I told her I liked Laura. I knew how these things were done. Everything was very codified, even with young kids like us. It was customary to write each other letters; that was the way of making contact with a girl. I grabbed a piece of paper and scribbled a few words, or rather a long declaration of love that took up several pages. I ended with a question of the type *Do you want to go out with me?* followed by two tick boxes marked *Yes* and *No*, and I even carefully added a postscript *Tick the correct box for your reply*. I went over to her, I crossed the playground and handed her the letter *I'll be waiting for your answer.* This phrase too was, along with the letter, part of the code.

Then I waited. She took her time to reply. I could see the signs of her hesitation, the way she would lower her eyes when I walked by. Days went by with no sign and no note. I knew why she didn't reply. There were moments when I would have liked not to say, not simply to say, but to scream at Laura in the middle of the playground, perched on a bench, a tree, wherever, to scream that she was a coward. That she didn't want to have anything to do with me because accepting my offer would have meant sharing my shame.

I persevered. I wrote more letters. In the end she accepted.

She sent me a few words by way of one of her friends. We agreed to meet in the roofed-in part of the school playground, after school but before everyone caught their bus. This was the area where couples met at the same time each day to make out. The student monitor had tried to chase everyone away at the beginning *Where do you think you are, this isn't the place to be kissing like that, for everyone to see. This is a school* but in the end she gave up.

Laura was waiting for me. She wasn't alone. People had heard, so others were there to witness the scene. They wanted to see me kiss a girl, to see if the gossip was true. I walked up, silent and trembling. I kissed her; I put my lips up against hers until I realised that she was trying to put her tongue in my mouth. I went along with it. The kiss lasted a few minutes – I was counting the seconds as they passed, wondering when this was going to end, and if, as a boy, I should take the initiative to end the kiss, take control, or wait. At the same time, I wanted the kiss to go on; I wanted it to be seen by the others, by as many eyes as possible, by crowds, by hordes of students. I wanted witnesses, so they'd all feel like idiots, so they'd be ashamed of the way they had covered me in opprobrium, so they'd think that all along they'd been making an absurd mistake, so they'd feel discredited and hurt by their mistake. The kiss ended and I walked off, wishing that I could run. I had found the whole exercise repulsive, foul.

On the bus I sat by myself and tried to get Laura's saliva and her smell out of my mouth, spitting quietly under my seat, rubbing my teeth and my tongue with my fingers to scrape off the odour that had stuck to them. I dreamed of putting an end to it. I thought of telling Laura the next day that it was already over. That evening when I met up with my cousin Stéphane he started asking me questions *Is it true, that you've got a girlfriend now, that Laura's your girl, the one everyone says is a real slut.* I noticed in his question a kind of admiration, of manly complicity that I had never shared with him before. It was even better for my reputation that I was going out with a *slut*. She transformed me in to a macho guy who had joined the set of guys-who-Laura-went-out-with. This conversation with my cousin made me change my mind.

And so I went on meeting Laura day after day before getting on the bus. More and more kids heard that we were going out. I would kiss her, and the kisses would last a long time, not only after school, but also during breaks, and in the morning when I saw her. I savoured the questions others asked me about her and me, about *being a couple*, about our *relationship*.

Laura wrote me letters and I made a point of leaving them in the pocket of my trousers so that my mother would find them when she did the laundry. One night when we were eating, she couldn't stop herself from saying something. Of course the ritual was that no one spoke during dinner; we all silently watched television or else my father would get angry *Put a sock in it! Zip it!* My mother: *So Eddy now that you found a girlfriend, you should learn to take better care of your love letters.* I pretended to be embarrassed. In reality, I was doing the best I could to hide the pride and joy that were bubbling inside me. At least for one evening I had managed to banish my mother's doubts. Her face looked relieved.

I would spend a couple hours on the telephone with Laura every night, making sure to warn my parents that I was going out that evening, so they wouldn't worry. My parents had no phone line and no Internet connection, as was true of the majority of people living in the village, and as is still the case for my mother as I write these lines. That meant that I had to go to the phone box near the bus stop for these calls with Laura. She would call me on her foster parents' phone.

At the bus stop I would find my *mates*. They'd say to come on over. It was so wonderful to be able to tell them that I couldn't because I had to talk with Laura, *my girl*, and then spend four, even five hours in the phone box talking to her, while they were right next door.

*

On one occasion when we were kissing in that roofed-in part of the playground, I noticed a warmth growing at the base of my spine. I felt myself getting an erection, and the longer we held the kiss, Laura and I, the harder I got. I was experiencing desire: a desire that was manifesting itself physically, one that you couldn't just imitate or fake. I had a hard-on, like when I was in the shed with my *mates*, like the men in the porn films that my father watched in his room, as he would let us know *I'm going into my room to watch some porn, so make sure none of you bothers me.* I had never felt aroused by a girl before. I thought I was succeeding at my project, that my body was giving in to my will. We are always playing roles and there is a certain truth to masks. The truth of my mask was this will to exist differently.

At last I was cured. On the way home, on the route from the school to my house, I revelled in my sense of victory, as if it were a refrain that I was listening to on a continuous loop, growing more powerful each time, not fading, since, to the contrary, I could feel my body was growing more and more excited, even wild. When I arrived home, I wondered if my parents could see the transformation (*I'm cured, I'm cured*). I told myself that perhaps bodies could go through sudden transformations, that perhaps my body had suddenly changed into a tough guy's, like my brothers'. I was sure they'd see a difference.

They didn't see a thing.

What I remember about the end of that afternoon: my heart pounding in my chest on the bus ride home (*I'm cured, I'm cured*), the rhythm of my breath, less, in fact, what you'd call a *respiratory rate* and more a series of suffocations, the tiny bits of gravel that were stuck under the door to the house and that made for a high-pitched squeak as I opened it. In my enthusiasm, I greeted my father *How's it going Dad?*

Shut the fuck up, I'm watching TV.

The body's rebellion

Blinded by the sense of having freed myself from what had seemed up until then to be an incurable disease, I forgot for a while the body's resistance. It hadn't occurred to me that wanting to change, or telling lies to yourself, wouldn't suffice to make the lies come true.

I was together in the playground with Laura when Dimitri came up to us. He was one of the truly tough guys, and he practically glowed with an unmatchable prestige thanks to his behaviour: insolence, bad marks, and all the rest. He spoke directly to Laura, pretending not to see me *Why are you going out with Eddy, I mean why go out with him when he's a homo. Everyone's saying the same thing, you're a homo's girlfriend.* A smile blanketed Laura's face, not at all a smile that was meant to hide some shame, I could tell, but rather a smile of complicity to let him know she didn't disagree with him, that she was aware of all that; other people had already told her. I lowered my head and, for a moment, felt like I wanted to apologise to her, to tell her I was sorry that I had made her share part of my burden.

It was moments like these that showed me the trap I was in, the impossibility of really changing while I was still inside the world of my parents, of school.

The ultimate betrayal by my body happened one night when I went to a club with a few of my *mates*. They were older than I was and had their driving licences; they'd say *Let's go to the club and pick up some girls, let's find some pussy tonight.*

They all took the driving test as soon as they were old enough, thinking it would set them free from the confines of the village, that they'd be able to travel (which they never did), to take short road trips (whereas they never went more than a few miles away to nearby nightclubs or to the ocean).

Often they would have to work for a whole summer at the factory – when they weren't already employed there – in order to be able to afford that precious square of pink paper. They didn't realise that this driving licence was, on the contrary, one of the many things, many factors, that kept them here. That now they would simply spend their nights drinking, not at the bus stop, but in their cars – where it was warmer, with the radio playing music. I had refused to take the exam, refused to go work for a month in the factory where I had finally promised myself I would never set foot. By the time I was eighteen I would in any case be far away from them.

On that night, the club – the place was called the Top Hat – was packed with hundreds of kids from all over the region, who formed an enormous compact and mobile mass that swallowed you up the moment you walked in. A local celebrity was giving a rap concert. In this moving crowd – moving in a way that made it seem like a single mass, a single immense body, like the body of a sluggish giant – people's sweaty bodies bumped and rubbed up against each other. Muscular bodies, most of them, smelling not only of sweat but of the cheap aftershave that I was also wearing.

I made my way towards the stage so I could see the singer who had managed to draw this crowd. Using my elbows, I was able to create a little space for myself near the stage that had been set up for the event. The ground was sticky because of all the drinks that had been spilled by the boys who were already pretty wasted and all jostling each other. Behind me was a man, much older, who had helped me make my way to my spot. I was probably the youngest person there, and he could see that. He had wanted to help me.

He was around thirty.

He was wearing an Airness tracksuit – just as many of the boys from my village or from nearby villages did on every kind of occasion, just as I had for a long time – since it was the brand everyone wanted then, with a cap stuck crooked on his shaved head, and a heavy, gold-coloured chain around his neck. His T-shirt had a wolf's head on it with an enormous snout. As I think back on it this T-shirt seems hideous and vulgar to me. But on the evening itself I found it pretty impressive.

He had the breath of an ox, heavy, scented (of pastis), and I felt it on the back of my neck.

The singer came out onstage; the crowd went wild and moved in tightly towards the stage. The man's body ended up pressed against mine, glued against mine, and each movement of the crowd rubbed our two bodies against each other. We were pressed more and more tightly together. He smiled, embarrassed and amused, his body giving off the odour of sweat.

I noticed a change in him, as he started to get an erection that went on getting harder and harder, knocking up against the base of my spine, as if following the beat, the rhythm of the music, each time a little bigger, a little harder. I could feel its shape precisely because of the tracksuit he was wearing.

I was overtaken by a fever that night.

Even though I hated the music I didn't move so that I could keep my body pressed up against his. After that evening I would go on listening to that same song over and over again in an attempt to reconstitute, at least in my thoughts and my dreams, the memory of that man. The lyrics have been engraved in me for ever:

> *Girl, sure you tell me you love me while I'm giving you*
> *all I've got as we dance together horizontally.*
> *Oh girl, we trip on hash so elegantly like no one can*
> *till we reach that peak and I give in to your deadly beauty*
> *It's Saturday night, I'm getting in the mood.*
> *I see a pretty young girl in the dark*
> *I go up to her, I say I'll buy her a drink*
> *She says, 'First let's get to know each other, show me what*
> *you've got.'*

When I got home, I tore off my clothes and started stroking myself, panting and moaning uncontrollably as I tried to be quiet: my sister was sleeping in the same room, in the bed underneath mine. My whole body, from my ears to the damp nape of my neck, including every pore of my skin, was shaken by my orgasm.

After that event, my body was always rebelling against me, reminding me what I really wanted, and demolishing all my ambitions to be like everyone else, to like girls the way everyone else did.

Often, after this night, on nights when I was alone in the house I would stretch out on my older brother's bed or on my own. My parents would go to the neighbours' to have a few drinks and the visit would last well into the night *We'll be back in five minutes, we're just going next door for a quick drink.* Soon they'd have run out of pastis and my father would take the car to go get more from the shop (*Really I drive better drunk than I do on an empty stomach*). My mother would call to tell me not to worry, they were just spending some time relaxing with the neighbours, *What else do you expect*, she would say, *what with the days your father has at the factory and me here doing housework all day long, I've earned a little time off* (then when my father lost his job – after the accident – my mother would say *With all the housework I have to do all day long and your father, sitting there in front of the TV, never moving, and me having to put up with him, I deserve a break*). I shouldn't worry and I could, if I wanted, make myself something to eat from the tins in the cupboard or the chips left over from lunch that I could warm up. She didn't realise that these evenings when they were gone were precious moments of freedom for me.

My brother hid porn magazines under his mattress. Everyone knew about it, and in fact he didn't really hide them, since he was in a certain way proud of them – just like my father who kept his X-rated films borrowed from Titi and Dédé in the kitchen cupboard where everyone could see.

Stretched out on my bed with the magazines, I'd find the photographs of naked women, their legs spread, their genitals on display, damp, sometimes with fingertips pressing on the fleshy lips to make them all the more visible and to make the clitoris stand out. Then their breasts, which I thought of as two excrescences, abnormal growths, masses filled with pus that you'd see on the bodies of sick people. Confronted with these naked women, I would squeeze my own genitals harder and harder, even imitating the back and forth motion of masturbation. I would spend entire hours, using all my concentration, thinking up every scene imaginable. My body would grow more and more damp, the clothes would be sticking to my body, drenched because of my furious efforts. I wanted, I ordered myself to have an orgasm even though I knew, because this is something I had known quite early, when I was quite young, I might even say that it is something I've always known, and that the opposite possibility never even occurred to me, I knew that it was the sight of a man's body that aroused me.

I never managed to come, not once, and because I tried so hard my penis, raw and blistered, would usually hurt for days afterwards.

A final attempt at love: Sabrina

Then Laura broke up with me in a letter. She had had enough of taking part in my shame and she must also have suffered from the distance I kept between us, despite myself, even if she couldn't quite explain it. A few weeks later she would meet another guy. It was a guy from the town where her mother lived, whom she went to visit a couple of times a year during school holidays. She would tell me about the evenings she spent with her new boyfriend, the films they would watch together before re-enacting certain sequences, the wild days in which they'd make love five or six times in a row, because they saw each other so rarely, the knightly exploits of this Kevin of hers, who broke another guy's nose *The guy whistled at me and said You're hot so Kevin went up to him, he told him You don't talk to my girl like that, you need to show her some respect. So then the guy answers him back and then all at once Kevin bashes his head in right in front of all these people who were looking out their windows.*

Without meaning to – or perhaps she intended more of it than I could tell – she let me know what I had been unable to do for her and with her. We had never made love, and I had never got into a fight over her. I was the one who got beaten up, not the one who picked the fights.

My older sister decided to introduce me to one of her friends. She said to me *At your age, you know you really need a girlfriend* and it's true I was at the age where most of the guys in the village were dating girls in the village, and were even becoming life-long couples, a status quickly confirmed by the birth of one or more children, which would mean they had to leave school. So my sister organised a dinner where I would meet this Sabrina. Having attained the impressive age of eighteen, Sabrina was five years older than I was, and therefore had a body that was considerably more developed than the bodies of the girls I knew at school. *And you know*, my sister added, *this way you'll be able to have a really good time*. I replied that I liked girls who were older than me, and added specifically *with curves*, knowing as I said this that I was unquestionably headed towards an impossible situation, one where, once I met Sabrina, I would have to live up to this image that I was presenting to my sister and to everyone else.

The dinner in question had been set up specifically so that we could meet. Sabrina's mother – Jasmine – was there. Jasmine was someone who hated her husband and openly declared that she couldn't wait for him to die *I don't know exactly when he'll finally die, but it's taking for fucking ever.* Once a week she visited a psychic who promised her that he was going to die of a violent illness in the very near future. I knew her for two years, and in those two years she would solemnly announce every week *It's really happening this time, my husband's finally about to die, I give him a month tops.* She would call up my sister and tell her *Get ready for the funeral, I just went to the psychic and he's only got seventy-two hours left to live.* Most of the conversation when she ate at our house dealt with the subject of his impending and unavoidable death, and with the details of the distribution of his tiny estate.

My sister had described me to Jasmine the same way that my father would when I wasn't around. She had told her that I was going to do really well in school and get rich. Jasmine, who wanted to see her daughter land on her feet, had quickly given her approval.

There was a ceremony in which we were formally introduced. I found myself face to face with my sister, Jasmine, Sabrina, and one of their other girlfriends, with all eyes on me and my anxiety as I imagined – the kind of absurd ideas that come to mind in moments like these – that Sabrina might throw her arms around me at any moment and try to kiss me. The palpable excitement that these four women were giving off matched precisely my uneasiness, an uneasiness that I tried to hide by projecting a false sense of confidence. I smiled at Sabrina and called attention to myself in any way I could, speaking about any and every topic I thought I knew something about, like, for example, the First World War, which I had just studied at school, and this seemed just fine with Jasmine, who would comment on what I was saying by turning to my sister *I like your little brother, I like him a lot, he's different.*

My sister, ready to try anything to make sure I hit it off with her friend, suggested as we were having a drink before dinner that I take Sabrina for a little walk. She gave me a knowing glance, as if this were something we had agreed upon earlier, and as if everything were unfolding exactly as we had planned. I responded with a similar glance, smiling slightly.

We headed down to the local park and we walked. My throat was painfully tight and dry. My heart was racing as I thought ahead to my sister's disappointment when she would learn from Sabrina that I hadn't been able to take any action, to act like a real guy, to flirt with her, and that I just stood there, immobile and inert, as passive – to invoke an expression my sister used and that I borrowed frequently – *as a ballsack in a tarpit.*

Before I was even able to get a word out, Sabrina spoke up and asked me to explain the reasons why I had wanted to get to know her. But I hadn't wanted to; it was a lie my sister had told her. I hid my astonishment when she asked the question and managed to offer a few platitudes, that I thought she was beautiful, that she was *my type*; what courage I found came from the certainty I had that Sabrina would report this conversation down to its tiniest details to the other girls, who might then start to think of me as a tough guy, a real man. She kissed me. She had to bend over slightly so that our lips could meet. The embrace lasted much too long, and I felt myself suffocating, losing my footing. As we were kissing, the effort required not to run off, not to cry out in disgust, became more and more intense. I couldn't let Sabrina see that I wanted it to be over as quickly as possible, because she could have told my sister.

We walked back up hand in hand to make the beginning of our relationship official to the other guests. My sister greeted us with satisfaction *How's it going lovebirds?* and everyone else applauded. I found this behaviour unseemly. I had grown up with and been shaped by these kinds of habits, these ways of behaving and yet they had already come to seem out of place to me – habits such as those found in my family: walking around the house naked, belching at the dinner table, not washing your hands before a meal. Being attracted to boys transformed my whole relationship to the world, encouraging me to identify with values that were different from my family's.

It was as if each clap of their hands tightened the chains between me and Sabrina, even though our relationship had barely begun.

It had been decided (I don't really remember by whom) that we should see each other every weekend at my sister's, and she would take us to a club on Saturday nights. At the club, I made a point of walking around with my arm round Sabrina, my latest conquest. I wanted to show the world, and myself, since I was watching everything I was doing and kept by far the closest eye on my own performance, not only that I was attracted to women, but that I was able to attract girls who were much older than I was.

Jasmine would bring Sabrina over to my sister's before we left for the club. She lived in a nearby village. As soon as she arrived, Jasmine would start by covering me with compliments. She said I was special, intelligent, that I would get her daughter to continue her education and earn lots of money. Sabrina wanted to become a midwife. She was different from the other girls in the village, most of whom wanted to become hairdressers, medical secretaries, sales assistants, teachers, if they were a bit more ambitious, or else to be housewives.

Sabrina's wish to study medicine provoked reactions of both amusement and scorn.

Listen to the stories that bimbo Sabrina tells about herself, thinking she's all special and better than the rest of us. Over time she gradually lowered her sights, just as my sister had done, from wanting to be a surgeon, to a general practitioner, then a nurse, then a nurse's aide, and then finally an in-home helper (making sure people took their medicine and *wiping old people's arses*, my mother's job).

Disgust

After a night at the club I would sleep at my parents' house and Sabrina would spend the night at my sister's. We would agree to meet up the next morning to go for a walk through the village streets and meet up with my *mates* at the bus stop, where they would be drinking before heading off to watch the Sunday football match.

After one of these nights at the club, my sister suggested that I sleep over at her house. Jasmine was coming to pick up Sabrina that night, because they were going on holiday, so Sabrina couldn't spend the night, and my sister didn't want to be alone; she hated that and said it made her afraid. Of course I agreed to her suggestion. I loved spending the night away from home: I felt ashamed of my parents' house because of its decrepit facade, and I hated my cold, damp room, which leaked on rainy days.

The window shutter had come loose in a violent storm one day and as it was yanked off it had shattered the window. After I told him (a long time after, since I told him the window was broken every day for weeks), my father put a piece of cardboard up to cover the hole left by the broken pane. He made a point of reassuring me *Don't worry, it's just until I have time to buy a pane of glass, it's temporary, it won't be like that for ever.* But he never fixed it.

The piece of cardboard would quickly get soaked with water. It was always having to be replaced. Yet no matter how attentive I was, how carefully I replaced the cardboard, water would get into my room. Dampness climbed up the walls, covered the cement floor, got into the wooden bed frames.

I slept on the top bunk above my sister, preferring to sleep in the upper bed so that I would be the one who got to climb up the small ladder. The bed would creak as I climbed up, but noises like that were to be expected, they didn't worry me, we knew they were because of the damp.

One night after I had climbed up as usual – with no indication that something was about to happen, the bed didn't squeak any more than normal – as I was stretching out, I felt the bed give way beneath my weight. The dampness had slowly caused the slats to deteriorate and, weakened, they finally broke. I landed a metre below, on top of my sister. She was injured by the broken slats. From that day forward my bed, no matter what repairs my father made, frequently collapsed on to my sister's.

*

So I was happy that she invited me to sleep over at her place, in her newly renovated little apartment.

We went out to the club, just as we'd been doing the past few weekends.

When we got home, my sister announced that she had to go meet a friend. It was at this moment that I understood what was happening, first of all because her story made no sense (why go meet a friend at five in the morning when you were exhausted and had just got home from a club, and all the streetlights in the village were out?), but also because she kept winking at me to let me know that she was lying. She added *That way you and Sabrina can both stay here, and, you know, her mum can just pick her up tomorrow*, which would save Jasmine from having to take the car out late at night in order to pick up her daughter and take her home; moreover, and more importantly, the two of us could sleep together in my sister's bed while she was at her girlfriend's house. Sabrina made next to no effort to hide the fact that she was in on this plan of my sister's, and even unpacked a few toiletries from her bag. Everyone knew what was up. I was the only one who had been left in the dark.

Once more I was a prisoner, terrified at the idea of spending the night with Sabrina, but caught in a situation where it was impossible for me to say anything, since any word could have destroyed my image. I knew what she expected from a night with me – given the difference in our ages and the more and more explicit references she had been making to the fact that we weren't yet having sex.

I winked back at my sister.

She left.

Sabrina and I went to bed – and I can no longer recall how I arranged things in order to speak to her as little as possible, to see as little as possible of her between the moment my sister left and the moment we got into bed. I kissed her with that vague sense of disgust that kissing always made me feel. I turned my back to her and rolled as far away from her as I could, finding myself at the edge of the bed, ready to fall out.

She came over to me to kiss some more. She took my hands and placed them on her breasts, then she slipped hers into my trousers. She started playing with my penis, which remained flaccid. I was unable to simulate being aroused. I tried to think of something else so that I could get an erection and so that Sabrina would be reassured, but the harder I concentrated the more improbable and distant any arousal seemed. She kept on, persevering with that small piece of flesh, as of yet barely surrounded by a light haze of blond pubic hair; she massaged and twisted it in every possible direction. At first I imagined making love to her, Sabrina, even while knowing there was no way such an image would get me hard. Then I imagined men's bodies pressing up against mine, muscled and hairy bodies colliding with mine, three, even four massive and brutal men. I thought of men holding down my arms so I couldn't move and then penetrating me with their dicks one by one, covering my mouth with their hands to keep me from making any noise. Men who would have pierced and torn at my body as if it were no more than a fragile piece of paper. I imagined the two boys, the tall redhead and the short one with the hunched back, making me grab their dicks, first with my hands, then with my lips, and finally with my tongue. I dreamed that they kept on spitting in my face, hitting me, and insulting me *faggot, poof* as they stuck their dicks in my mouth, not one by one but both together, suffocating me, almost making me vomit.

Nothing did any good. Every time Sabrina touched my skin it reminded me of the truth of what was happening, of her woman's body and my detestation of it. I pretended to have a sudden and severe asthma attack. I said that I had to go right home to my parents' house, that I was having an asthma attack, and that it was possible, as my grandmother's recent death had shown, that it really was possible to die from such an attack.

The next day I broke up with Sabrina. She wept when I told her but I remained cold as ice.

A first attempt at flight

With Sabrina I had failed, losing the battle between my desire to become a tough guy, and the desire of my own body, which was pushing me towards men, which is to say pushing me away from my family, away from the whole village. And yet I didn't want to give up, so I continued repeating to myself that obsessive phrase, *Today I'm gonna be a tough guy.* My failure with Sabrina made me redouble my efforts. I took care to make my voice deeper, still deeper. I kept my hands immobilised in my pockets whenever I spoke, so I wouldn't wave them around. Following the night that had revealed to me more clearly than ever the impossibility of my becoming aroused by a woman's body, I took a more serious interest in football than ever before. I began watching it on television and memorised the names of all the players on the French team. I watched wrestling as well, just like my brothers and my father. I made my hatred of gay people ever more explicit in order to deflect suspicion.

*

It must have been towards the end of my last year at the collège. There was another boy, even more effeminate than I was, and people called him *Trout Lips*. I hated him because he didn't share in my suffering, he didn't seem interested in sharing it, he never made any effort to get to know me. Yet mixed with this hatred was a sense of closeness, of finally having someone around me who was like me. I was fascinated by him and on a few occasions I had tried to go up to him (but only when he was alone in the library, because I couldn't be seen talking to him). He kept his distance.

One day he was being loud in a hallway where a large group of students had gathered, and I called out *Shut the fuck up faggot*. All the students laughed. Everyone looked at him and looked at me. I had managed, for the moment of an insult shouted in a hallway, to transfer my shame to him.

As the months went by, following the two boys' departure for the lycée, their disappearance from the collège, and thanks to all the energy I put into my efforts to be a tough guy, insults grew rare, both at school and at home. But the rarer they became, the more violent they felt, the more difficult each one was to endure, leaving me feeling melancholy for days, or even weeks. Although they were less frequent, the insults continued for a long time despite my furious effort to be more masculine, because they were based not on how I appeared then, but on the way I had been perceived for years and that was well established in people's minds.

Running away was my only chance, it was all I had left.

I've wanted to show here that my flight was not the result of a project that I had had in mind for a long time, as if I were some kind of a creature struggling for freedom, as if I had always wanted to escape, but rather that escape was the only option left to me after a series of defeated attempts to change who I was. Flight was at first something I experienced as a kind of failure, something to which I resigned myself. Back then, to succeed would have meant being like everyone else. But I had tried everything.

I didn't know how to go about it. I had to learn. People talk as if what makes it hard to run away is that you feel homesick, or that you are attached to people or to other aspects of your life, but no one mentions that it can be hard to do because you simply don't know how to do it. At first my attempts were clumsy and ridiculous.

My parents were grilling some meat in the back yard shortly after I had broken up with Laura. I headed off to my room coming up with a plan to leave. My father had just said something cruel to me because I had refused to look after the barbecue coals, for fear of burning myself *You really are a pussy.* In my room I gathered up some belongings and threw them into a rucksack. I had decided to run away for ever. I was never coming back.

My little brother came in. He was young, maybe five years old, probably less. He asked me what I was doing and I told him I was leaving for good, hoping that he would go, as he usually did, and tell my parents what I had said. But he didn't budge. He just stood there, without moving. So I tried again, repeating myself, varying my intonation in an effort to make him understand that I was doing something that was forbidden. *I'm leaving. I'm going away for ever.* He didn't understand. I tried yet again. Still no reaction. In the end, I made him an offer I knew he wouldn't refuse. I offered to give him some sweets (*some treats* is what I said) if he would tell on me. He left the room. I heard his footsteps fading away, and his voice crying *Daddy, Daddy.* I left the house at a run, slamming the door behind me so that my father would hear and understand that my little brother was telling the truth.

I ran through the streets of the village, carrying my rucksack – setting my pace so that my father would be able to follow me, feeling him a few dozen metres behind me. He yelled my name only once, so that no one would hear and there wouldn't be any kind of a scandal with the women talking about us outside the school the next day, *tongues wagging.* I hid behind a bush. He ran right past me, without seeing me. He hadn't seen me. Suddenly I was terrified that he'd lose my trail and leave me there. Would I have to spend the night outdoors? In the cold?

What would I eat? What would happen to me? I coughed loudly so that he would hear.

He turned and saw me. He grabbed me by the hair *You little shit, you little fucking moron, what the hell do you think you're doing, you little arsehole.* He grabbed the sleeves of my T-shirt and shook me so hard that it tore.

Later my mother would tell this story while laughing *Oh my God that day your dad really gave you what you had coming but you just stood there and took it.*

He dragged me back to the house by my arm, on which he had a fierce grip. He sent me to my room where I cried, and I was still crying when he came in several hours later. He sat down at the foot of the bed. You could smell the alcohol (my mother the next day: *What with you running away it went to his head even quicker than usual, it really got to him, your running off*). Then he started crying *You can't do shit like that, you know we love you, you can't just run away.*

Strait is the gate

I had to get away.

At this point I was in the last year of collège, and it was time to decide what stream I would follow. I absolutely refused to go to the nearby lycée in Abbeville as would have been usual. I wanted to get far away from my parents and I didn't want to run into the two boys again. The idea was to end up somewhere new, saying to myself – this was my hope given the progress I had made – that people wouldn't think of me as a faggot there. I could start over from the beginning, I could be reborn. My theatrical experience in the collège drama club offered me an unforeseen way out. I had put a lot of effort into the theatre. This was partly because it annoyed my father and because I was already beginning, at that age, to define everything I did in relation to (in opposition to) him. It was also because, since I showed some talent for acting, theatre was a source of validation for me. I would try anything to get people to like me *That Bellegueule kid really cracks you up when he's onstage in the play at the end of the school year.* It made my big sister proud *Maybe you can be the next Brad Pitt.*

I remember one night we were putting on a show in the village hall near the collège at the end of the school year, a little play that I had written for the occasion. It was a kind of a cabaret piece where different characters followed each other on to the stage and introduced themselves, told their story, and sang a song. I was playing the role of Gérard, an alcoholic whose wife had left him, who was on his way to being homeless, and who sang

Germaine, Germaine
Let's do a waltz, let's do a tango
Either one, you know
Means I love you
And I love my Kanterbrau, ow, ow, ow.

I remember that the two boys were in the audience that night. They were off at the lycée by this point, but they must have come to see the other kids in their family, or else they just came for fun.

I remember the fear I felt when I saw them, imagining that they'd be waiting for me when I left. The hall was small, which meant I could see their faces clearly even in the dark. I performed my act, terrified that they might yell out *faggot* during a moment of silence, in between two lines, in front of my mother and everyone else. Somehow I made it through to the end. When I was finished, they both stood up and yelled exuberantly *Bravo Eddy, bravo!*

They started chanting my name *Eddy, Eddy* until all the villagers present joined in, around three hundred of them who were all suddenly chanting my name, clapping their hands in rhythm and staring at me with delight. Getting everyone to quieten down was difficult. When it was time for the curtain calls and I was onstage with all the other members of the troupe, they started calling out my name again. I didn't see them after the show. I think that was the last time in my life that I ever saw them.

The head teacher came to see me after one of my classes to speak to me about Madeleine-Michelis Lycée, which was in Amiens, the largest city in our area, and one I had barely ever visited because I was too frightened. My father always said, over and over, that there were lots of coloured people there, and that they were dangerous *Amiens is full of black people, Ay-rabs, towelheads, you go there and it's like being in Africa. Best to stay away, you'll just get robbed if you go.* He had always said these kinds of things to me, and even if I told him that he was just being racist – making a point of always contradicting him, being different from him – still his words managed to leave me feeling uneasy.

*

Madeleine-Michelis Lycée had a theatre programme leading to the baccalaureate. You had to take an exam to get in, and then turn in an application and audition. When the head teacher, Mrs Coquet, suggested that I try for a place, I had never really even thought of attempting to get a baccalaureate, even less of aiming for a stream that prepared you for university. No one in my family had done this, no one in the village either, except maybe for the children of the schoolteachers, the mayor, or the woman who owned the shop. I mentioned it to my mother; she barely knew what we were talking about (*Oh so now the intellectual in the family is aiming to take the bac*).

I worked with the head teacher's daughter, a young actress, to prepare the scene for my audition. Her mother allowed me to skip lessons and gave us permission to use a classroom. I worked until I was exhausted. I couldn't let this chance to escape slip through my fingers. I could board at this lycée, which meant putting even more distance between me and the village.

My mother warned me *You're only going to your drama school if they pay for room and board cause we can't pay, so otherwise you go to Abbeville, one lycée is the same as another.* And then my father *I don't see why you can't go to Abbeville like everyone else, you're always needing to be different.*

It was no easy task to convince my father to take me to the train station on the day of the audition *Wasting petrol*

for this theatre shit of yours, really why should I. The train
station was ten miles from the village. For several days he
insisted there was no way he would take me to the station
and that there was no point in getting my hopes up. On
the last night he changed his mind *Tomorrow don't forget to
set your alarm, I'm driving you to the station.*

He would do this kind of thing often, saying *no* right up
to the last minute, and only giving way after I'd given him
the satisfaction of watching me cry and beg for hours
on end. He enjoyed it. When I was seven or eight years
old, for no apparent reason he gave my stuffed animal –
the one I slept with and carried with me everywhere, as
all children do – to the neighbour's children. I screamed
and carried on, hollering all around the house. He sat and
watched with a smile on his face. On 31 December 1999,
on the Feast of Saint Sylvester, New Year's Eve, he told
me that at midnight an asteroid was going to strike the
earth and we were all going to die. No one would survive. *Make sure you enjoy life right now because before you
know it we're all gonna die.* My tears flowed all night long. I
moaned, not wanting to die. My mother protested, saying
he couldn't treat me that way on New Year's Eve, leaving
me sitting on the steps of the house feeling miserable,
unable to enjoy the new millennium. She tried to reassure
me *Don't you listen to your dad, he's making it all up,
come watch TV with us, they'll show the Eiffel Tower.* It made
no difference; I only believed my father's words; he was

the man of the house. That night too, the communal room in our house would echo with his laughter.

The next morning he walked by my bedroom half an hour before the time we had agreed on *Get your arse out of bed. If we're early you can wait at the station.* I ran to the bathroom to get ready. I didn't brush my teeth. My father wasn't in the bathroom, since he never washed in the morning. He just put on a T-shirt and a pair of trousers and splashed some water on his face, then he lit a cigarette and sat down in front of the television to watch the news or the shopping channel.

Once we were in the car, we had an hour to cover fifteen kilometres. We said nothing to each other. To break the awkward silence, I asked him to turn on the radio. He knew all the songs by the famous French singers, and belted them out. Sometimes between two songs he'd start up again *To think I dragged my own arse out of bed at this hour for this theatre shit of yours, I mean really . . .* (My mother: *Your father is always complaining but don't pay any attention, he doesn't mean it. It's just his way of passing the time and because he doesn't know what else to say.*)

At the station he told me to get out of the car, then changed his mind and told me to wait. I was looking at him, surprised, waiting for him to say something disagreeable. He stuck his hand in his pocket and pulled out a twenty-euro note. I knew this was far too much, more than he could or should be giving me. He told me I'd need it *You'll be needing to eat lunch. I don't want you feeling ashamed in front of any of the others or feeling different cause you don't have enough money. You spend all of this this morning, you don't bring any back with you, I don't want you to be any different than the others. But you watch out, cause there'll be lots of Arabs around. If one of them looks at you, you just look down, you don't try to be smart, don't you be any kind of a big shot, cause people like that always have their cousins or their brothers hanging around nearby so if you start something they're all there to gang up on you, and you're dead. If there's one of them who asks you for money, you give him everything. Your wallet, your phone, everything. What matters is staying alive. Now get going and don't fuck up the audition.*

I took the train to Amiens. I was nervous, expecting a gang of Arabs to appear at every station and steal all my belongings.

To get to Michelis Lycée I walked fast and kept my head down. Each time a black person or an Arab walked on the same side of the street as me – although there weren't really that many of them – I would be gripped with fear.

There were others waiting in the hallway with their parents. I was happy to be alone; it made me feel more grown up – and I was also bitter, jealous of these other young people who seemed so much a part of a closely knit family. I thought their parents themselves seemed somehow like teenagers when they spoke to their children, as if the happiness of their lives were reflected in the gentleness of their character.

A tall man with white hair stepped out of the room where the auditions were taking place and called out my name *Bellegueule, your turn.* Everyone else laughed. Even the grown-ups. Bellegueule. Prettymug. This was the first part of the selection process, before I performed the scene I had prepared. I had to answer questions about the theatre and why I wanted to come to this lycée. I had thought about all my answers well ahead of time: my passion for the theatre, the importance of art in our society and throughout history, my wish to broaden my horizons. A bunch of clichés.

The teacher who was interviewing me, the man with the white hair, Gérard, who would become my drama teacher once I got in, did not share my experience of this admissions interview. He would confide in me two years later – with his characteristic quiet irony – that I had begged him to admit me to the school. That I practically got down on my knees. He imitated me: *Please sir, help me get out of where I am, for God's sake.* He told me I never stopped smiling. It didn't seem natural to him, but he was moved by the strong will, or perhaps we should call it desperation, that emanated from me. He told me that I had done the same thing in the second part of the admissions process, while performing my scene *There was an imploring quality in your voice at every moment.*

During the audition process I met a young man named Fabrice. We chatted and promised that we would be friends that autumn if we were both admitted. Fabrice haunted my thoughts all summer. In truth, I was thinking less about Fabrice himself than about the possibility that I could have a circle of friends in Amiens, friends who were boys, as a boy should have, and not just friends who were girls any more.

All summer long I waited for the letter to arrive that would let me know if I had been accepted. There was no sign of it. My parents assured me that they hadn't received anything *Stop asking, you're driving us crazy.*

Nothing. I was in a state of despair. I finally resigned myself: they hadn't even bothered to let me know they had rejected me. I lay awake all night imagining I would have to go to the lycée in Abbeville, run into the two boys again and relive the same scenes from collège.

I began to think of dropping out.

After supper with my parents one night, in early or mid-August, I was watching television in my room, when my father called me into the main room.

He announced that he had received a letter about a month ago, but he hadn't thought to show it to me until now. As he said this his face took on an amused expression that let me know he wasn't telling me the truth, that he had hidden the letter so that I would have to lie around waiting all summer.

I grabbed the letter *Monsieur Bellegueule, Madeleine-Michelis Lycée is pleased to inform you . . .*

A second later I was running out of the house. I barely had time to hear my mother say *What is that crazy fool up to now?*

I didn't want to be around them; I refused to share this moment with them. I was already far away; I had already left their world behind; that's what the letter had told me. I went off into the fields and walked for most of the night, in the cool of the North, on the dirt paths, with the odour of rapeseed, strong at that time of year, all around me.

The entire night was spent imagining my new life far from here.

Epilogue

A few weeks later,

My departure.

I have prepared myself for boarding school

It's not a big suitcase

but a large gym bag that had belonged first to my brother
and then to my sister.

My clothes too, most of them, are hand-me-downs from
my brother and my sister, some from my cousins.

When I arrive at the station,

the fear of black people and Arabs isn't as bad as it was
before.

I want to be far away from my father already, far away
from them

and I know that this begins with turning all my values
upside down.

The place where I board is not at Michelis Lycée itself.

It is further away, on the south side of the city.

A little more than two kilometres

I didn't know this, so I arrived at the lycée with my navy
blue sports bag and Mr Royon, the Dean of Students,
laughed
*Oh no, my boy, your dorm is on the other side of town. You need
to take the bus, bus number 2.*

My mother didn't give me money for the bus fare.
She didn't know either
I walk along the side of the road
I stop the passers-by
Excuse me, excuse me, can you tell me how to find . . .
No one will answer
I see the annoyance and the worry on their faces.
They think I'm going to ask them for money.

I find the dormitory at last –
my fingers are raw, nearly bloody from walking those
kilometres while carrying my suitcase, my bag.
Now I remember, there is even a pillow in a plastic bag
that I am carrying under my arm.
I must seem ridiculous, people must be mistaking me for
a homeless person

At the dormitory I am told that I'll be in a room by
myself, separate from the other boarders.
I will see very little of those other boarders.
The dormitory is part of a different lycée, but they have
agreed to house me.

Too overjoyed to be disappointed

I tell myself that the dormitory isn't important, that I will meet my friends at my lycée, that the dorm is just something that helps me get that much further away

The first days of the school year,

Loneliness,

Everyone already knows everyone else, they come from the same collèges.

And yet they still talk to me

Do you want to sit with us at lunch today, what's your name again, Eddy?

That's a strange-sounding name, Eddy, is it a nickname?

Isn't your full name Édouard?

Bellegueule, man, that's quite a name, Bellegueule,

do people make fun of it a lot?

Eddy Bellegueule, holy shit, Eddy Bellegueule, what an unbeliev-able name

Now I learn –

something I had already suspected,

that had already crossed my mind.

Here boys kiss each other on each cheek when they say *bonjour*, they don't shake hands

They carry leather satchels

They have gentle manners

They would all have been called *fags* at my collège

Bourgeois people don't exhibit the same kind of bodily
 habits
They don't define virility the way my father did, the way
 the men at the factory did
(this will be even more apparent at the École Normale,
 all those feminine bodies belonging to middle-class
 intellectuals)

And that's exactly what I say to myself at first when I see
 them
I say to myself
What a bunch of fucking faggots
Which is also a kind of relief
*Maybe I'm not gay, maybe things aren't the way I thought they
 were,*
*maybe I've just always had a bourgeois body that was trapped in
 the world of my childhood*

I don't run across Fabrice, as he is in a different class,
but I'm not worried, I didn't specifically want him, but
 what he represented.
I get to know Charles-Henri, and he becomes my best
 friend, I spend time with him
We talk about girls

Other people in our class say
*You know Eddy and Charles-Henri, you never see one without
 the other*

I love hearing them say that

I wish they'd say it more often, and louder,

that they'd go to my village.

and that they'd announce there, so that everyone could
   hear

Eddy has a best friend, a boy

They talk about girls, about basketball

(Charles-Henri was teaching me how to play)

They even play hockey

And yet I notice that Charles-Henri is beginning to slip
   away from me

There are other boys he has more fun with,

the ones who are as good at sports as he is, who have
   played for ever

who play music, like he does

Who probably talk about girls better than I do

Holding on to his friendship is a battle

One morning,

it's in December, two months into the school year

Some of the students are wearing Santa Claus hats

I'm wearing the jacket that we bought especially for me
   to take to the lycée

Bright red and yellow, an Airness jacket. I felt so proud
   when we bought it, my mother had said

quite proud herself

It's your present to take to the lycée, it's really expensive, we're
   pinching pennies so we can afford it
But as soon as I got to the lycée, I realised that it didn't
   fit in with the people here, that no one here wore
   things like that; the boys wore men's coats or else wool
   jackets, like hippies wore
People found my jacket comical
Three days later, filled with shame, I threw it in a bin.
My mother will cry when I lie to her (*I lost it*).

We are gathered in the hallway, in front of the door to
   room 117, waiting for the teacher, Mrs Cotinet.
Someone walks up,
Tristan.
He calls out to me
Hey Eddy, as gay as ever?
Everyone laughs.

I laugh along with them.